CHILDREN'S THRIFT CLASSICS

Little Women

LOUISA MAY ALCOTT

Adapted by Bob Blaisdell
Illustrated by Thea Kliros

DOVER PUBLICATIONS, INC.
Mineola, New York

DOVER CHILDREN'S THRIFT CLASSICS
GENERAL EDITOR: STANLEY APPELBAUM
EDITOR OF THIS VOLUME: ADAM FROST

Bibliographical Note

This Dover edition, first published in 1997, is a new abridgment of a standard text of *Little Women*. The introductory Note and the illustrations were prepared specially for this edition.

Library of Congress Cataloging-in-Publication Data

Alcott, Louisa May, 1832–1888.
  Little women / Louisa May Alcott ; adapted by Bob Blaisdell ; illustrated by Thea Kliros.
    p.   cm. — (Dover children's thrift classics)
  Summary: An abridged version of the classic novel chronicling the joys and sorrows of the four March sisters as they grow into young women in nineteenth-century New England.
  ISBN 0-486-29634-2 (pbk.)
  [1. Sisters—Fiction.   2. Family life—New England—Fiction.   3. New England—Fiction.]   I. Blaisdell, Robert.   II. Kliros, Thea, ill.   III. Title.   IV. Series.
PZ7.A335Li   1997
[Fic]—dc21   96-39462
                                                                        CIP
                                                                        AC

Manufactured in the United States of America
Dover Publications, Inc., 31 East 2nd Street, Mineola, N.Y. 11501

Note

LOUISA MAY ALCOTT (1832–1888) was one of four daughters of the educator and social reformer Bronson Alcott. Her father was an impractical man, filled with idealistic plans that did little to support his family; by the time she was in her mid-teens, Louisa had been obliged to go to work in order to supplement the family's income. She worked as a domestic, as a teacher and then as a writer, beginning with sensational thrillers that she wrote under a pseudonym, and later turning to domestic novels, of which this book is one.

In writing *Little Women* (1868–1869), her first children's book, Alcott drew on her childhood experiences, modeling the characters of Jo and the other March girls upon herself and her own sisters. The book's instant success freed the Alcotts from their financial difficulties and won the author recognition and acclaim; it was to be the first in an enormously popular series. The present volume highlights the struggles and the triumphs of the March family, retelling the basic story of *Little Women* in a way that is sure to charm young readers.

Contents

Chapter 1

A Letter

CHRISTMAS WON'T be Christmas without any presents," grumbled Jo.

"It's so dreadful to be poor!" sighed Meg.

"I don't think it's fair for some girls to have plenty of pretty things, and other girls nothing at all," added little Amy.

"We've got Father and Mother and each other," said Beth.

The four young faces brightened at the cheerful words, but darkened again as Jo said sadly, "We haven't got Father, and shall not have him for a long time." Each thought of Father far away down South, where the fighting against the rebels was.

Then Meg said, "You know the reason Mother proposed not having any presents this Christmas was because it is going to be a hard winter for everyone, and she thinks we ought not to spend money for pleasure when our men are suffering so in the army. We can't do much, but we can make our little sacrifices, and ought to do it gladly."

"But I don't think the little we would spend would do any good. We've each got a dollar, and the army wouldn't be much helped by our giving that. I agree not to expect anything from Mother or you, but I do want to buy a new novel for myself," said Jo, who was a bookworm.

"I planned to spend mine on new music," said Beth.

"I shall get a nice box of drawing pencils; I really need them," said Amy.

"Mother didn't say anything about our money, and she won't wish us to give up everything. Let's each buy what we want, and have a little fun; I'm sure we work hard enough to earn it," cried Jo.

1

"I know *I* do—teaching those tiresome children nearly all day when I am longing to enjoy myself at home," said Meg.

"You don't have half such a hard time as I do," said Jo. "How would you like to be shut up for hours with a nervous, fussy old lady, who keeps you trotting, is never satisfied and worries you till you're ready to fly out of the window or cry?"

"It's naughty to fret, but I do think washing dishes and keeping things tidy is the worst work in the world. It makes me cross, and my hands get so stiff, I can't practice piano well at all," said Beth.

"I don't believe any of you suffer as I do," cried Amy, "for you don't have to go to school with rude girls, who tease you if you don't know your lessons, and laugh at your dresses and at your father if he isn't rich."

"Don't you wish we had the money Papa lost when we were little, Jo? Dear me! how happy and good we'd be, if we had no worries!" said Meg.

"You said, the other day, you thought we were a deal happier than the King children, for they were fighting and worrying all the time, in spite of their money."

"So I did, Beth," said Meg. "Well, I think we are; for, though we do have to work, we make fun for ourselves."

"True," said Jo, "but it's bad to be a girl, anyway, when I like boys' games and work and manners! I'm dying to go and fight in the war with Papa, and I can only stay at home and knit, like a poky old woman!"

"Poor Jo! You must try to be contented with making your name boyish, and playing brother to us girls," said Beth.

The four sisters sat knitting away in the twilight, while the December snow fell quietly outside, and the fire crackled cheerfully in the room. It was a comfortable old room, though the carpet was faded and the furniture was very plain; for a good picture or two hung on the walls, books filled the shelves, and chrysanthemums and Christmas roses bloomed in the windows.

Margaret, or Meg, the eldest of the four, was sixteen, and very pretty, with large eyes, plenty of soft, brown hair, and a

The four sisters sat knitting away in the twilight.

sweet mouth. Fifteen-year-old Jo was very tall, thin, and reminded one of a colt, for she never seemed to know what to do with her long arms and legs, which were very much in her way. She had a determined mouth, a comical nose, and sharp, gray eyes. Her long, thick hair was her one beauty, but it was usually bundled in a net, to be out of her way. She had round shoulders and big hands and feet. Elizabeth, or Beth, as everyone called her, was a rosy, smooth-haired, bright-eyed girl of thirteen, with a shy manner, a timid voice and a peaceful expression. She seemed to live in a happy world of her own, only leaving it to meet the few whom she trusted and loved. Amy, the youngest, was a regular snow maiden, with blue eyes, yellow hair curling on her shoulders, pale and slender.

When Mr. March lost his property in trying to help an unfortunate friend, the two oldest girls begged to be allowed to do something towards their own support, at least. Believing that they could not begin too early to cultivate energy, industry and independence, their parents consented. Margaret found a place as nursery governess, and felt rich with her small salary. As she said, she *was* "fond of luxury," and her chief trouble was poverty. She found it harder to bear than the others, because she could remember a time when home was beautiful, life full of ease and pleasure, and want of any kind unknown.

Jo happened to suit Aunt March, who was lame and needed an active person to wait upon her. Something in Jo's comical face and blunt manners struck the old lady's fancy, and she proposed to take her as a companion. This did not suit Jo at all, but she accepted the place since nothing better appeared, and, to everyone's surprise, got on remarkably well with her cranky relative.

I suspect that Jo's real attraction there was a large library of fine books, which was left to dust and spiders since Uncle March died. Jo remembered the kind old gentleman, who used to let her build railroads and bridges with his big dictionaries. The dim, dusty room, with the sculpted busts staring down from the tall bookcases, the cozy chairs, the globes and, best of all, the wilderness of books in which she could wander where she liked, made the library a place of bliss to her. The moment Aunt March took her nap or was busy with company, Jo hurried to this quiet spot, and curling herself up in the easy chair, devoured poetry, romance, history, travels and pictures.

Beth was too bashful to go to school; it had been tried, but she suffered so much that it was given up, and she did her lessons at home with her father. Even when he went away, and her mother was called on to devote her skill and energy to Soldiers' Aid Societies, Beth went on by herself, and did the best she could. She was a housewifely little creature, and helped their servant Hannah keep home neat and comfortable, never thinking of any reward but to be loved. Long, quiet days she spent, but not lonely or idle, for her little world was peopled with imaginary friends, and she was by nature a busy bee. There were six dolls to be taken up and dressed every morning.

Beth had her troubles as well as the others, and not being an angel but a very human little girl, she often "wept a little weep," as Jo said, because she couldn't take music lessons and have a fine piano. She loved music so dearly, she practiced away patiently at the jingling old piano that wouldn't keep in tune. She sang like a little lark, and never was too tired to play for Marmee (Mother) and the girls.

If anybody had asked Amy what the greatest burden of her life was, she would have answered, "My nose." It was not big, nor red; it was only rather flat. No one minded it but herself, and it was doing its best to grow.

Amy had a talent for drawing, and was never so happy as when copying flowers, designing fairies or illustrating stories. Her teachers complained that, instead of doing her math, she covered her slate with animals. She got through her lessons as well as she could. She was a great favorite with her mates, being good-tempered. She could play twelve tunes, crochet and read French without mispronouncing all of the words. She had a sad way of saying, "When Papa was rich we did so-and-so," which was very touching, and her long words were considered "perfectly elegant" by the girls.

Meg was Amy's confidante and adviser, and, by some strange attraction of opposites, Jo was gentle Beth's. To Jo alone did shy Beth tell her thoughts. The two elder girls, Meg and Jo, were a great deal to one another, but each took one of the younger into her keeping, and watched over her in her own way, "playing mother" they called it.

The clock struck six, and, having swept up the hearth, Beth put a pair of their mother's slippers down to warm.

"They are quite worn out; Marmee must have a new pair," said Jo.

"I thought I'd get her some with my dollar," said Beth.

"No, I shall!" cried Amy.

"I'm the oldest," began Meg, but Jo cut in, saying, "I'm the man of the family, now Papa is away, and I shall buy the slippers, for he told me to take special care of Mother while he was gone."

"I'll tell you what we'll do," said Beth. "Let's each get her something for Christmas, and not get anything for ourselves."

"Let Marmee think we are getting things for ourselves, and then surprise her. We must go shopping tomorrow afternoon, Meg. There is so much to do about the play for Christmas night," said Jo.

And then they rehearsed this play, which Jo herself had written, and which left the girls in high spirits.

"Glad to find you so merry, my girls," said a cheery voice at the door, and the actors turned to welcome a tall, motherly lady. She was not elegantly dressed, but the girls thought the gray cloak and unfashionable bonnet covered the most splendid mother in the world.

"Well, dearies, how have you got on today? There was so much to do, getting the boxes ready to go tomorrow, that I didn't come home till now. Has anyone come calling, Beth? How is your cold, Meg? Jo, you look tired to death. Come and kiss me, baby."

While asking these questions, Mrs. March got her wet clothes off, her warm slippers on, and sitting down in the easy chair, drew Amy to her lap, preparing to enjoy the happiest hour of her busy day. The girls flew about, trying to make things comfortable, each in her own way.

As they gathered about the table, Mrs. March said, "I've got a treat for you after supper."

A quick, bright smile went round like a streak of sunshine. Jo cried out, "A letter! a letter! Three cheers for Father!"

"Yes, a nice long letter. He is well, and thinks he shall get through the cold season better than we feared. He sends all sorts of loving wishes for Christmas, and a special message to you girls," said Mrs. March.

"I think it was so splendid of Father to go as chaplain when he was too old to be drafted, and not strong enough for a soldier," said Meg.

"Don't I wish I could go as a drummer, or a nurse, so I could be near him and help him!" exclaimed Jo.

"It must be very unpleasant to sleep in a tent, and eat all sorts of bad-tasting things, and drink out of a tin mug," sighed Amy.

"Now come and hear the letter."

"When will he come home, Marmee?" asked Beth.

"Not for many months, dear, unless he is sick. He will stay and do his work as long as he can, and we won't ask him back a minute sooner than he can be spared. Now come and hear the letter."

They all drew to the fire, Mother in the big chair, with Beth at her feet, Meg and Amy perched on either arm of the chair, and Jo leaning on the back. Father said little of the hardships he suffered; it was a cheerful, hopeful letter, full of lively descriptions of camp life, marches and war news, and only at the end did his heart overflow with love:

"Give them all my dear love and a kiss. Tell them I think of them during the day and pray for them at night. A year seems very long to wait before I see them, but remind them that while we wait we may all work, so that these hard days need not be wasted. I know they will remember all I said to them, that they will be loving children to you, will do their duty, fight their enemies bravely, and conquer themselves so beautifully, that when I come back to them, I may be fonder and prouder than ever of my little women."

Everybody sniffed when they came to that part. Amy hid her face on her mother's shoulder and sobbed out, "I *am* a selfish girl! but I'll truly try to be better, so he mayn't be disappointed in me."

"We all will!" cried Meg. "I think too much of my looks, and hate to work, but won't any more, if I can help it."

"I'll try and be what he loves to call me, 'a little woman,' and not be rough and wild, but do my duty here instead of wanting to be somewhere else," said Jo, thinking that keeping her temper at home was a much harder task than facing a rebel or two down South.

Beth said nothing, but wiped away her tears, and began to knit with all her might, losing no time in doing her duty.

Chapter 2

A Merry Christmas

JO WAS the first to wake Christmas morning. The winter sunshine crept in to touch the bright heads and faces with a Christmas greeting.

"Where is Mother?" asked Meg, as she and Jo ran downstairs.

"Goodness only knows. Some poor creature come a-beggin', and your ma went straight off to see what was needed. There never *was* such a woman for givin' away vittles and drink, clothes and firewood," replied Hannah, who had lived with the family since Meg was born, and was considered by them all more as a friend than a servant.

"She will be back soon, I think, so fry your cakes, and have everything ready," said Meg, looking over the presents which were collected in a basket and kept under the sofa, ready to be given at the proper time.

"There's Mother. Hide the basket, quick!" cried Jo, as a door banged, and the girls rushed to the table, eager for breakfast.

"Merry Christmas, Marmee!" they cried, in chorus.

"Merry Christmas, little daughters! I want to say one word before we sit down. Not far away from here lies a poor woman with a little newborn baby. Six children are huddled into one bed to keep from freezing, for they have no fire. There is nothing to eat over there at the Hummels', and the oldest boy came to tell me they were suffering hunger and cold. My girls, will you give them your breakfast as a Christmas present?"

They were all unusually hungry, having waited nearly an hour, and for a minute or two no one spoke.

Then Jo exclaimed, "I'm so glad you came before we began!"

"May I go and help carry the things to the poor little children?" asked Beth.

"I shall take the cream and the muffins," added Amy, giving up the food she most liked.

Meg was already covering the buckwheats, and piling the bread into one big plate.

"I thought you'd do it," said Mrs. March, smiling. "You shall all go and help me, and when we come back we will have bread and milk for breakfast, and make it up at dinnertime."

How the big eyes stared as the girls went in!

They were soon ready, and they set out through back streets, arriving to find a poor, bare, miserable room, with broken windows, no fire, ragged blankets, a sick mother, crying baby and a group of hungry children cuddled under one old quilt, trying to keep warm.

How the big eyes stared and lips smiled as the girls went in!

"Oh, my God, it is good angels come to us!" said the poor woman, crying for joy.

That was a very happy breakfast, though the girls didn't get any of it; and when they all went away, leaving comfort behind, I think there were not four merrier people than the hungry little girls who gave away their breakfasts and contented themselves with bread and milk on Christmas morning.

"That's loving our neighbor better than ourselves, and I like it," said Meg, as they set out their presents, while their mother was upstairs collecting clothes for the poor Hummels.

"She's coming down! Start playing the piano, Beth! Open the door, Amy! Three cheers for Marmee!" cried Jo, prancing about, while Meg went to lead Mother to the seat of honor.

Beth played her most cheerful march, and Amy threw open the door. Mrs. March was both surprised and touched; she smiled with her eyes full as she examined her presents, and read the little notes which accompanied them. The slippers went on at once, a new handkerchief was placed into her pocket, a rose was fastened in her bosom, and two nice new gloves were pronounced a "perfect fit."

There was a good deal of laughing and kissing and explaining, in the simple, loving fashion which makes these home festivals so pleasant at the time, so sweet to remember long afterwards, and then all fell to work, preparing for the evening festivities. The girls put their wits to work, and made whatever they needed for their Christmas play.

No gentlemen were admitted, so Jo played male parts to her heart's content. The smallness of the company made it necessary for her and Meg to take several parts apiece, and they certainly deserved credit for the hard work they did in learning their lines, whisking in and out of various costumes, and managing the stage besides.

On Christmas night, a dozen girls, friends of the March sisters, went upstairs to a bedroom transformed into a theater, and piled onto the bed, which was the "dress circle," and sat before the blue and yellow homemade curtains. There was a good deal of rustling and whispering behind the curtain, and an occasional giggle from Amy, who was apt to get hysterical. Soon a bell sounded, the curtains flew apart, and the *Operatic Tragedy* began.

It was a long, complicated play, but very satisfying, and the audience of girls gave it tremendous applause when it was over.

From this excitement, the girls were invited by Mrs. March to come down to supper. This supper was a surprise, even to the actors, and, when they saw the table, they looked at one another in amazement. It was like Marmee to get up a little treat for them, but anything so fine as this was unheard of since the departed days of plenty. There was ice-cream—actually two dishes of it, pink and white—and cake and fruit and bonbons, and, in the middle of the table, four great bouquets of hothouse flowers.

It quite took their breath away; and they stared first at the table and then at their mother.

"Is it fairies?" asked Amy.

"It's Santa Claus," said Beth.

"Mother did it," said Meg, smiling her sweetest.

"Aunt March had a *good* fit, and sent the supper," cried Jo.

"All wrong. Old Mr. Laurence sent it," replied Mrs. March.

"The Laurence boy's grandfather! What in the world put such a thing into his head? We don't know him!" exclaimed Meg.

"Hannah told one of his servants about your breakfast party. He is an odd old gentleman, but that pleased him. He knew my father, years ago, and he sent me a polite note this afternoon, saying he hoped I would allow him to express his friendly feeling towards my children by sending them a few trifles in honor of the day. I could not refuse, and so you have a little feast at night to make up for the bread-and-milk breakfast."

"That boy put it into his head, I know he did! He's a capital fellow, and I wish we could get acquainted. He looks as if he'd like to know us, but he's bashful, and Meg is so prim she won't let me speak to him when we pass," said Jo.

"You mean the people who live in the big house next door, don't you?" asked one of Meg's friends. "My mother knows old Mr. Laurence, but says he's very proud, and doesn't like to mix with his neighbors. He keeps his grandson shut up, when he isn't riding or walking with his tutor, and makes him study very hard. We invited him to a party, but he didn't come. Mother says he's very nice, though he never speaks to us girls."

"Our cat ran away once, and he brought her back, and we talked over the fence, and were getting on capitally when he saw Meg coming and walked off. I mean to know him some day, for he needs fun, I'm sure he does," said Jo.

"I like his manners, and he looks like a little gentleman; so I've no objection to your knowing him, if a proper opportunity comes. He brought the flowers himself, and I should have asked him in, if I had been sure what was going on upstairs. He looked so sad as he went away, hearing the fun, and evidently having none of his own."

They looked at one another in amazement.

"It's a mercy you didn't, Mother!" laughed Jo. "But we'll have another play sometime that he *can* see. Perhaps he'll help act; wouldn't that be jolly?"

"I never had such a fine bouquet before! How pretty it is!" And Meg examined her flowers with great interest.

"They *are* lovely. But Beth's roses are sweeter to me," said Mrs. March, smelling the half-dead flower in her belt.

Beth nestled up to her, and whispered softly, "I wish I could send my bunch to Father. I'm afraid he isn't having such a merry Christmas as we are."

Chapter 3

The Laurence Boy

Jo! Jo! Where are you?" cried Meg, at the foot of the attic stairs.

"Here!" answered Jo's voice from above, and, running up, Meg found her sister eating apples and crying over *The Heir of Redclyffe,* wrapped up in a comforter on an old sofa by the sunny window. This was Jo's refuge, and here she loved to come with half a dozen apples and a nice book, to enjoy the quiet and the society of a pet rat who lived near by and didn't mind her a bit. As Meg appeared, Scrabble whisked into his hole. Jo shook the tears off her cheeks and waited to hear the news.

"Such fun! only see! a regular note of invitation from Mrs. Gardiner for tomorrow night!" cried Meg, waving the precious paper and then proceeding to read it.

"'Mrs. Gardiner would be happy to see Miss Margaret and Miss Josephine at a little party on New Year's Eve.' Marmee is willing we should go, now what *shall* we wear?"

"What's the use of asking that, when you know we shall wear poplins because we haven't got anything else?" answered Jo.

"If I only had a silk!" sighed Meg.

"I'm sure our poplins look like silk, and they are nice enough for us. Yours is as good as new, but I forgot the burn and the tear in mine. Whatever shall I do? The burn shows badly."

"You must sit still all you can and keep your back out of sight; the front is all right. I shall have a new ribbon for my hair, and Marmee will lend me her little pearl pin, and my new slippers are lovely, and my gloves will do, though they aren't as nice as I'd like."

"My gloves are spoiled with lemonade, and I can't get any new ones, so I shall have to go without," said Jo.

"You *must* have gloves, or I won't go," cried Meg. "Gloves are more important than anything else. Can't you make them do?"

"I can hold them crumpled up in my hand, so no one will know how stained they are; that's all I can do. No, I'll tell you how we can manage—each wear one good one and carry a bad one."

"Your hands are bigger than mine, and you will stretch my glove dreadfully," said Meg.

"Then I'll go without. I don't care what people say!" cried Jo.

"You may have it, you may! Only don't stain it, and do behave nicely."

"Don't worry about me. I'll be as prim as I can, and not get into any scrapes, if I can help it. Now go and answer your note, and let me finish this splendid story."

On New Year's Eve the parlor was deserted, for upstairs the two younger girls played dressing maids, and the two older were absorbed in the all-important business of "getting ready for the party." They looked very well in their simple outfits—Meg in silvery drab, with a blue velvet snood, lace frills and the pearl pin; Jo in maroon, with a stiff linen collar and a white chrysanthemum or two. Each put on one nice light glove, and carried one soiled one, and all said the effect was "quite easy and fine." Meg's high-heeled slippers were very tight and hurt her, though she would not say so, and Jo's nineteen hairpins all stuck straight into her head, which was not exactly comfortable; but, dear me, let us be elegant or die!

"Have a good time, dearies!" said Mrs. March, as the sisters went down the walk. "Don't eat much supper, and come away at eleven when I send Hannah for you." And the gate clashed behind them.

"Now don't forget to keep the bad side of your dress out of sight, Jo," said Meg, as she turned from the mirror in Mrs. Gardiner's dressing room.

"I know I shall forget. If you see me doing anything wrong just remind me by a wink, will you?" said Jo.

"No, winking isn't ladylike; I'll lift my eyebrows if anything is wrong, and nod if you are all right. Now hold your shoulders straight, and take short steps, and don't shake hands if you are introduced to anyone: it isn't the thing."

"How do you learn all the proper ways? I never can," said Jo.

In they went then to the party, feeling a trifle timid, for they seldom went to parties, and, informal as this little gathering was, it was an event to them. Mrs. Gardiner, a proper old woman, greeted them kindly, and handed them over to the eldest of her six daughters. Meg knew Sallie, and was at her ease very soon, but Jo, who didn't care much for girls or girlish gossip, stood about, with her back carefully against the wall, and felt as much out of place as a colt in a flower garden. Half a dozen boys were talking about skates in another part of the room, and she longed to go and join them, for skating was one of the joys of her life. She signaled to Meg what she wanted to do, but Meg's eyebrows went up so alarmingly that she dared not stir. No one came to talk to her, and one by one the group near her dwindled away, till she was left alone. She could not roam about and amuse herself, for the burnt side of her dress would show, so she stared at people rather sadly till the dancing began. Meg was asked at once, and the tight slippers skipped about so briskly that no one would have guessed the pain their wearer suffered. Jo saw a big red-headed boy approaching her corner, and fearing he meant to ask her to dance, she slipped behind a curtain and into a small room, intending to peep and enjoy herself in peace. Unfortunately, another bashful person had chosen the same place, for, as the curtain fell behind her, she found herself face to face with the "Laurence boy."

"Dear me, I didn't know anyone was here!" stammered Jo.

But the boy laughed and said pleasantly, "Don't mind me; stay if you like."

"Shan't I disturb you?"

"Not a bit; I only came here because I don't know many people, and I felt rather strange at first, you know."

"So did I. Don't go away, please, unless you'd rather."

The boy sat down again and looked at his shoes, till Jo said, trying to be polite:

"Dear me, I didn't know anyone was here!"

"I think I've had the pleasure of seeing you before. You live near us, don't you?"

"Next door!" he said, laughing.

She laughed too, and said, "We did have such a good time over your nice Christmas present."

"Grandpa sent it."

"But you put the idea into his head, didn't you, now?"

He smiled, but changed the subject, asking, "How is your cat, Miss March?"

"Nicely, thank you, Mr. Laurence; but I am not Miss March, I'm only Jo," answered the young lady.

"I'm not Mr. Laurence, I'm only Laurie."

"Laurie Laurence—what an odd name!"

"My first name is Theodore, but I don't like it, for the fellows called me Dora, so I made them say Laurie instead."

"I hate my name, too—so sentimental! I wish everyone would say Jo, instead of Josephine. How did you make the boys stop calling you Dora?"

"I thrashed 'em."

"I can't thrash Aunt March, so I suppose I shall have to bear it," sighed Jo. In a moment, she asked, "Do you like parties?"

"Sometimes; you see, I've been in Europe a good many years, and haven't been in company enough yet to know how you do things here."

"Europe!" cried Jo. "Oh, tell me about it! I love dearly to hear people describe their travels."

Laurie didn't seem to know where to begin, but Jo's eager questions soon set him going, and he told her how he had been at school in Vevey, where the boys never wore hats and had a fleet of boats on the lake, and for holiday fun went on walking trips about Switzerland with their teachers.

Both peeped through the curtains and chatted, till they felt like old acquaintances. Laurie's bashfulness soon wore off, for Jo's manner set him at his ease, and Jo was her merry self again, because her dress was forgotten, and nobody lifted their eyebrows at her. She liked the "Laurence boy" better than ever and took several good looks at him, so that she might describe him to the girls.

"Curly black hair, brown skin, big black eyes, handsome nose, fine teeth, small hands and feet, taller than I am, very polite, for a boy, and altogether jolly. I wonder how old he is?"

She asked in a roundabout way, "I suppose you are going to college soon? From our garden I see you at your window studying hard at your books."

Laurie smiled, and answered, "Not for a year or two; I won't go before seventeen, anyway."

"Are you only fifteen?" asked Jo, looking at the tall lad, whom she had imagined seventeen already.

"Sixteen, next month."

"How I wish I was going to college!"

"I don't. Nothing but grinding away or playing around."

"What do you like?"

"To live in Italy, and to enjoy myself in my own way."

Jo wanted to ask what his own way was, but he looked troubled now, so she changed the subject by saying, as her foot tapped to the music, "That's a splendid polka in the next room. Why don't you go and try it?"

"If you will come too," he answered, with a bow.

"I can't; for I told Meg I wouldn't because—" There Jo stopped, and looked undecided whether to tell or to laugh.

"Because what?" asked Laurie.

"You won't tell?"

"Never."

"Well, I have a bad habit of standing before the fire, and so I burn my frocks, and I scorched this one, and though it's nicely mended, it shows, and Meg told me to keep still, so no one would see it. You may laugh, if you want to; it is funny, I know."

But Laurie didn't laugh. He said very gently, "Never mind that. Please come."

Jo thanked him and gladly went.

When the music stopped, they sat down; Laurie was in the middle of telling of a students' festival when Meg appeared in search of her sister. She beckoned, and Jo got up and followed her into a side room, where Meg sat down on a sofa, holding her foot and looking pale.

"I've sprained my ankle. That stupid high heel turned and gave me a sad wrench. It aches so I can hardly stand, and I don't know how I'm ever going to get home," she said, rocking to and fro in pain.

"I knew you'd hurt your feet with those silly shoes. I'm sorry. But I don't see what you can do, except get a carriage, or stay here all night," answered Jo, softly rubbing the poor ankle as she spoke.

"I can't have a carriage without its costing ever so much. I can't stay here, for the house is full. I'll rest till Hannah comes, and then do the best I can."

"I'll ask Laurie; he will go," said Jo.

"Mercy, no! Don't ask or tell anyone. Get me my overshoes, and put these slippers with our things. As soon as supper is over, watch for Hannah, and tell me the minute she comes."

When Hannah appeared and was told the news, Jo slipped outside, ran down, and, finding a servant, asked if he could get her a carriage. He knew nothing about the neighborhood, however, and Jo was looking round for help when Laurie, who had heard what she said, came up and offered his grandfather's carriage, which had just come for him.

"It's so early! You can't mean to go yet?" began Jo.

"I always go early—I do, truly! Please let me take you home. It's on my way."

That settled it; and, telling him of Meg's mishap, Jo gratefully accepted, and rushed up to bring down the rest of their group. They then rolled away in the luxurious carriage, feeling very festive and elegant. Laurie went up outside the carriage beside the driver, so Meg could keep her foot up, and the girls talked over their party in freedom.

Jo told her adventures, and by the time she had finished they were at home. With many thanks to Laurie, they said good night and crept in.

Chapter 4

Being Neighborly

W HAT IN the world are you going to do now, Jo?" asked Meg, one snowy afternoon, as her sister came tramping through the hall, in rubber boots, old sack and hood, with a broom in one hand and a shovel in the other.

"I can't keep still all day and, not being a pussycat, I don't like to doze by the fire. I like adventures, and I'm going to find some."

Meg went back to toast her feet and read, and Jo began to dig paths. The snow was light, and with her broom she soon swept a path all round the garden, for Beth to walk in when the sun came out and Beth's dolls needed air. The garden separated the Marches' house from that of Mr. Laurence. Both stood in a suburb of the city, which was still countrylike, with groves and lawns, large gardens and quiet streets. A low hedge parted the two estates. On one side was an old, brown house, looking rather bare and shabby, robbed of the vines that in summer covered its walls, and the flowers which then surrounded it. On the other side was a stone mansion, showing every sort of comfort and luxury. Yet it seemed a lonely, lifeless sort of house, for no children played on the lawn, no motherly face ever smiled at the windows, and few people went in and out, except the old gentleman and his grandson.

To Jo, this fine house seemed a kind of enchanted palace, full of delights which no one enjoyed. She had long wanted to see its hidden glories, and to know better the "Laurence boy." Since the party, she had been more eager than ever, and had planned many ways of making friends with him; but he had not been seen lately, and Jo began to think he had gone away, when she one day spied a brown face at an upper window, looking sadly down into their garden, where Beth and Amy were snowballing each other.

"That boy needs friends and fun," she said to herself. "His grandpa does not know what's good for him, and keeps him shut up all alone. He needs somebody to play with. I've a mind to go over and tell the old gentleman so."

The plan of "going over" was not forgotten, and when the snowy afternoon came, Jo decided to try what could be done.

The head turned at once.

She saw Mr. Laurence drive off, and then went out to dig her way down to the hedge, where she paused and looked over. All quiet—curtains down at the lower windows, servants out of sight, and nothing human visible but a curly black head leaning on a thin hand at the upper window.

"There he is," thought Jo, "poor boy! All alone and sick this dismal day. I'll toss a snowball and make him look out, and then say a kind word to him."

Up went a handful of snow, and the head turned at once. Jo laughed and waved her broom as she called out:

"How do you do? Are you sick?"

Laurie opened the window, and croaked out, "Better, thank you. I've had a bad cold, and been shut up a week."

"I'm sorry. What do you amuse yourself with?"

"Nothing; it's as dull as tombs up here."

"Don't you read?"

"Not much; they won't let me."

"Can't somebody read to you?"

"Grandpa does, sometimes, but my books don't interest him and I hate to ask Brooke all the time."

"Have someone come and see you, then."

"There isn't anyone I'd like to see. Boys make such a noise, and my head is weak."

"Isn't there some nice girl who'd read and amuse you? Girls are quiet and like to play nurse."

"Don't know any."

"You know us," said Jo.

"So I do! Will you come, please?" cried Laurie.

"I'm not quiet and nice, but I'll come, if Mother will let me. I'll go ask her. Shut that window, like a good boy, and wait till I come."

With that, Jo shouldered her broom and marched into her house. A few minutes later, Laurie heard someone being shown to the door of his little parlor. Jo appeared looking rosy and kind, with a covered dish in one hand and Beth's three kittens in the other.

"Here I am, bag and baggage," she said. "Mother sent her love, and was glad if I could do anything for you. Meg wanted me to bring some of her sweet pudding, and Beth thought her cats would be comforting."

It so happened that Beth's loan was just the thing, for in laughing over the cats, Laurie forgot his bashfulness, and grew sociable at once.

"How kind you are! Now please take the big chair, and let me do something to amuse you," said Laurie.

"No. I came to amuse you. Shall I read aloud?" and Jo looked towards some books near by.

"Thank you! I've read all those, and if you don't mind I'd rather talk," answered Laurie.

"I'll talk all day if you'll only set me going. Beth says I never know when to stop."

"Is Beth the rosy one, who stays at home a good deal, and sometimes goes out with a little basket?" asked Laurie.

"Yes, that's Beth."

"The pretty one is Meg, and the curly-haired one is Amy, I believe?"

"How did you find that out?"

Laurie answered, "Why, you see, I often hear you calling to one another, and when I'm alone up here, I can't help looking over at your house, you always seem to be having such good times. I beg your pardon for being so rude, but sometimes you forget to put down the curtain at the window; and when the lamps are lighted, it's like looking at a picture to see the fire, and you all round the table with your mother. It looks so sweet, I can't help watching. I haven't got any mother, you know."

"You may look as much as you like," said Jo. "I just wish, though, instead of peeping, you'd come over and see us. Mother is so splendid, she'd do you heaps of good, and Beth would sing to you if I begged her to, and Amy would dance; Meg and I would make you laugh over our funny plays, and we'd have jolly times. Wouldn't your grandpa let you?"

"I think he would, if your mother asked him. He's very kind, though he does not look so, and he lets me do what I like, pretty much, only he's afraid I might be a bother to strangers," said Laurie.

"We are not strangers, we are neighbors, and you needn't think you'd be a bother. We want to know you, and I've been trying to do so such a long time. We haven't been here a great while, you know, but we have got acquainted with all our neighbors but you."

"You see, Grandpa lives among his books, and doesn't mind much what happens outside. Mr. Brooke, my tutor, doesn't stay here, you know, and I have no one to go about with me, so I just stay at home."

"That's bad. You ought to make an effort, and go visiting everywhere you are asked; then you'll have plenty of friends, and pleasant places to go to."

Jo then told him about her work with Aunt March, and gave him a lively description of the fidgety old lady, her fat poodle, the parrot that talked Spanish, and the library she loved. She went on and told all about her sisters and herself, of their plays and plans, their hopes and fears for Father, and the most interesting events of the little world in which the sisters lived. Then they got to talking about books, and to Jo's delight, she found that Laurie loved them as well as she did, and had read even more than herself.

"If you like them so much, come down and see ours. Grandpa is out, so you needn't be afraid," said Laurie.

"I'm not afraid of anything," returned Jo.

Jo clapped her hands and pranced.

"I don't believe you are," exclaimed the boy.

Laurie led the way from room to room, letting Jo stop to examine whatever struck her fancy; and so at last they came to the library, where she clapped her hands and pranced. It was lined with books, and there were pictures and statues and little cabinets full of coins and curiosities, and chairs and strange tables, and, best of all, a great open fireplace.

"What richness!" sighed Jo, sinking into a chair and gazing about her. "Theodore Laurence, you ought to be the happiest boy in the world."

"A fellow can't live on books," said Laurie.

Before he could say more, a bell rang, and Jo exclaimed, "Mercy me! It's your Grandpa!"

"Well, what if it is? You are not afraid of anything, you know," returned the boy.

"I think I am a little bit afraid of him, but I don't know why I should be. Marmee said I might come, and I don't think you're any the worse for it," said Jo.

A maid came in and said, "The doctor to see you, sir."

"Would you mind if I left you for a minute?" said Laurie to Jo.

"Don't mind me. I'm as happy as a cricket here," answered Jo.

Laurie went away, and his guest amused herself in her own way. She was standing before a fine portrait of the old gentleman when the door opened again, and, without turning, she said, "I'm sure now that I shouldn't be afraid of him, for he's got kind eyes, though his mouth is grim, and he looks as if he had a tremendous will of his own. He isn't as handsome as my grandfather, but I like him."

"Thank you, ma'am," said a gruff voice behind her, and there, to her great dismay, stood old Mr. Laurence.

Poor Jo blushed, but then as she looked at the living eyes under the bushy gray eyebrows, she saw they were kinder even than the painted ones. The old gentleman said, "So you're not afraid of me, hey?"

"Not much, sir."

"And you don't think me as handsome as your grandfather?"

"Not quite, sir."

"And I've got a tremendous will, have I?"

"I only said I thought so."

"But you like me, in spite of it?"

"Yes, I do, sir."

That answer pleased the old gentleman; he gave a short laugh, shook hands with her, and, putting his fingers under her chin, said, "You've got your grandfather's spirit, if you haven't his face. He *was* a fine man, my dear; but, what is better, he was a brave and honest one, and I was proud to be his friend."

"Thank you, sir."

"What have you been doing to this boy of mine, hey?" was the next question.

"Only trying to be neighborly, sir." And Jo told how her visit came about.

"You think he needs cheering up a bit, do you?"

"Yes, sir, he seems a little lonely, and young folks would do him good perhaps. We are only girls, but we should be glad to help if we could, for we don't forget the splendid Christmas present you sent us," said Jo.

"Tut, tut, tut. That was the boy's affair. Oh, there's the tea bell. Come down and go on being neighborly."

At tea, the old gentleman saw how his grandson and Jo chatted away like old friends. There was color, light and life in the boy's face now.

"She's right, the lad *is* lonely. I'll see what these little girls can do for him," thought Mr. Laurence. He liked Jo, for she seemed to understand the boy almost as well as if she had been one herself.

After old Mr. Laurence had come by to visit, said something funny or kind to each one of the girls, and talked over old times with their mother, nobody felt much afraid of him, except timid Beth.

Then the new friendship flourished like grass in spring. Everyone liked Laurie, and he informed Brooke, his tutor, that "the Marches were regular splendid girls." They took the lonely boy into their midst and made much of him, and he found something very charming in the companionship of these girls. What good times they had! Such plays and sleigh rides and skating parties, such pleasant evenings in the old parlor, and now and then such fine little parties at the great house. Meg could walk in the conservatory whenever she liked, Jo browsed over the new library, and Amy copied pictures and enjoyed beauty to her heart's content.

But Beth, though yearning to play the grand piano, could not pluck up courage to go to the "Mansion of Bliss," as Meg called it. She went once with Jo, but the old gentleman's voice frightened her away, and she declared she would never go there any more. Nothing could change her mind, till Mr. Laurence, hearing of her fear, set about mending matters. During one of the brief calls he made on the Marches, he led the conversation to music and talked away, fascinating Beth. At the back of his chair she stood listening, with her great eyes wide open and her cheeks red. Mr. Laurence talked on about Laurie's lessons and teachers; and then, as if the idea had just occurred to him, he said to Mrs. March:

"The boy neglects his music now, and the piano suffers for want of use. Wouldn't some of your girls like to run over and practice on it now and then, just to keep it in tune, you know, ma'am? They needn't see or speak to anyone, but run in at any time; for I'm shut up in my study at the other end of the house, Laurie is out a great deal, and the servants are never near the drawing room after nine o'clock. Please tell the young ladies what I say, and if they don't care to come, why, never mind."

Here he rose, as if going, and Beth made up her mind to speak.

"Oh, sir, they do care, very, very much." She slipped her hand into his, and looked up at him with gratitude.

"Are you the musical girl?" he asked.

"I love it dearly, and I'll come if you are quite sure nobody will hear me—and be disturbed," she said.

"Not a soul, my dear. The house is empty half the day; so come and drum away as much as you like, and I shall be obliged to you."

"How kind you are, sir!"

Beth blushed, but she was not frightened now, and gave the big hand a grateful squeeze, because she had no words to thank him for the gift he had given her.

The old gentleman, stooping down, kissed her, saying, "I had a little granddaughter once, with eyes like yours. God bless you, my dear!" And away he went, in a great hurry.

The next day, having watched both the old and the young gentlemen leave their house, Beth, after two or three retreats, sneaked in at the side door and made her way to the drawing room where the piano stood. With trembling fingers and frequent stops to listen and look about, Beth at last touched the great instrument, and right away forgot her fear. The delight which the music gave her was like the voice of a beloved friend.

After that, she slipped through the hedge nearly every day, and the great drawing room was haunted by a musical spirit that came and went unseen. She never knew that Mr. Laurence often opened his study door to hear the old songs he liked. She enjoyed herself heartily, and found that her granted wish was all that she had hoped.

"Mother," she said one day, "I'm going to make Mr. Laurence a pair of slippers. He is so kind to me, I must thank him, and I don't know any other way. Can I do it?"

"Yes, dear. It will please him very much, and be a nice way of thanking him."

Beth was a nimble little needlewoman, and the slippers were finished soon. Then she wrote a very short, simple note, and, with Laurie's help, got them left on the study table one morning before the old gentleman was up.

All that day passed, and a part of the next, before any answer arrived, and she was beginning to fear she had offended her friend. On the afternoon of the second day, she went out to do an errand. As she came up the street, on her return, she saw four heads popping in and out of the parlor windows, and the moment they saw her, several joyful voices screamed:

"Here's a letter from the old gentleman! Come quick, and read it!"

Beth hurried on in a flutter. At the door, her sisters seized and bore her to the parlor, all pointing, and all saying at once, "Look there! Look there!" There stood a little upright piano, with a letter lying on the glossy lid, directed to "Miss Elizabeth March."

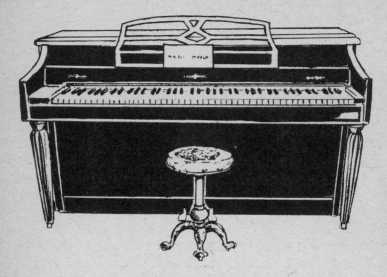

There stood a little upright piano.

"For me?" gasped Beth.

"Yes, all for you, my precious," said Jo. "Don't you think he's the dearest old man in the world?"

The letter read:

"MISS MARCH:

"I have had many pairs of slippers in my life, but I never had any that suited me so well as yours. I like to pay my debts, so I know you will allow 'the old gentleman' to send you something which once belonged to the little granddaughter he lost. With thanks and best wishes, I am

"Your grateful friend and humble servant,

"JAMES LAURENCE."

"Laurie told me how fond Mr. Laurence used to be of the child who died, and how he kept all her little things carefully," said Jo.

"Try it, honey. Let's hear the sound of the baby pianny," said Hannah.

So Beth tried it, and everyone said it was the most remarkable piano ever heard.

"You'll have to go and thank him," said Jo, by way of a joke, for the idea of the child's really going never entered her head.

"Yes, I mean to. I guess I'll go now, before I get frightened thinking about it." And, to the amazement of the family, Beth walked down the garden, through the hedge, and in at the Laurences' door.

She went and knocked at the study door; when a gruff voice called out, "Come in!" she did go in, right up to Mr. Laurence, and held out her hand, saying, "I came to thank you, sir, for—" But she didn't finish, for he looked so friendly that she forgot her speech, and, only remembering that he had lost the little granddaughter he loved, she put both arms round his neck and kissed him.

Chapter 5

Camp Laurence

GIRLS, WHERE are you going?" asked Amy, finding them secretly getting ready to go out.

"Never mind. Little girls shouldn't ask questions," said Jo sharply.

Amy was determined to find out the secret. Turning to Meg, she said, "Do tell me! I should think you might let me go, too."

"I can't, dear," began Meg, but Jo broke in, "You can't go, Amy, so don't be a baby."

Amy saw Meg slip a fan into her pocket.

"I know! You're going with Laurie to the theater!" she cried. "I *shall* go, for Mother said I might, and I've got money."

"That isn't proper when you weren't asked. So you just stay where you are," scolded Jo.

Amy began to cry and Meg to reason with her, when Laurie called from below, and the two girls hurried down. Just as the party was setting out, Amy called down, "You'll be sorry for this, Jo March!"

"Fiddlesticks!" said Jo.

They had a charming time, for the play was as wonderful as anyone could imagine. But Jo's pleasure had a drop of bitterness in it, and she wondered what her sister would do to make her "sorry for it."

When they got home, they found Amy reading in the parlor. She had an injured air about her, and she never asked a question about the play. But Jo could not find any evidence that her sister had made good her promise, and she decided that Amy had forgiven her.

There Jo was mistaken, for the next day she made a discovery which produced a tempest. Meg, Beth and Amy were sitting together when Jo burst into the room, demanding, "Has anyone taken my book?"

Meg and Beth said, "No," at once, but Amy said nothing. Jo was upon her in a minute.

"Amy, you've got it!"

"No, I haven't."

"You know where it is, then!"

"No, I don't."

"That's a fib!" cried Jo. "You know something about it, and you'd better tell at once."

"You'll never see your silly old book again," said Amy. "I burned it up. I told you I'd make you pay for being so cross yesterday, so—"

Amy got no further, for Jo's hot temper mastered her, and she shook Amy, crying, "You wicked, wicked girl! I shall never be able to write it again, and I shall never forgive you as long as I live!"

Meg flew to rescue Amy, and Beth to pacify Jo, but Jo was beside herself and rushed out of the room.

Amy was soon brought to see the wrong she had done her sister. Jo's book was the pride of her heart; it was only half a dozen little fairy tales, but she had worked over them patiently, hoping to make something good enough to print. Amy's bonfire had destroyed the work of several years.

When the tea bell rang, Jo appeared, looking so grim that it took all of Amy's courage to say: "Please forgive me, Jo. I'm very, very sorry."

"I never shall forgive you," was Jo's answer, and from that moment she ignored Amy completely.

It was not a happy evening, for the sweet home peace was disturbed.

As Jo received her good-night kiss, Mrs. March whispered, "My dear, forgive each other and begin again tomorrow."

Jo shook her head and said, because Amy was listening, "It

was an abominable thing, and she doesn't deserve to be for-given."

Jo still looked like a thundercloud in the morning, and nothing went right all day. "Everybody is so hateful, I'll ask Laurie to go skating. He will put me to rights," said Jo to herself, and off she went.

Amy heard the clash of skates and looked out.

"There! she promised she would take me next time, for this is the last ice we shall have. But it's no use to ask such a cross girl to take me."

"Don't say that. You *were* very naughty, and it *is* hard to forgive the loss of her book; but I think she might do it now, if you ask her at the right minute," said Meg.

"I'll try," said Amy, and she ran after the friends.

Jo saw her coming and turned her back. Laurie did not see, for he was skating along the shore, sounding the ice. As he turned the bend, he shouted back: "Keep near the shore; it isn't safe in the middle."

Jo heard, but Amy was struggling to put on her skates and did not catch a word. Jo glanced over her shoulder and thought: "No matter whether she heard or not, let her take care of herself."

Laurie had vanished around the bend, Jo was just at the turn, and Amy, far behind, striking out toward the ice in the middle of the river. For a minute Jo stood still; then she resolved to go on, but something turned her round, just in time to see Amy throw up her hands and go down, with a sudden crash of rotten ice and splash of water. She tried to call Laurie, but her voice was gone; she tried to rush forward, but her feet seemed to have no strength in them. Something rushed by her, and Laurie's voice cried out: "Bring a rail. Quick, quick!"

For the next few minutes she worked as if possessed, blindly obeying Laurie, who held Amy up till Jo dragged a rail from the fence. Together they got the child out, more frightened than hurt.

Shivering, dripping and crying, they got Amy home, and she fell asleep before a hot fire. When Amy was comfortably asleep, Mrs. March called Jo to her.

Amy went down with a crash of rotten ice.

"Are you sure she's safe?" whispered Jo.

"Quite sure, dear," replied her mother cheerfully.

"Mother, if she *should* die, it would be my fault." And Jo dropped down beside the bed in tears. "It's my dreadful temper! I try to cure it, and then it breaks out worse than ever. Oh, Mother, what shall I do?"

"Remember this day, and resolve with all your soul that you will never know another like it. I am angry nearly every day of my life, Jo, but I have learned not to show it."

The patience and the humility of the face she loved so well was a better lesson to Jo than the wisest lecture, the sharpest reproof. She felt comforted by the sympathy given her, and, as if eager to begin at once to mend her fault, Jo looked up with an expression on her face which it had never known before.

"I wouldn't forgive her, and today, if it hadn't been for Laurie, it might have been too late! How could I be so wicked?" said Jo.

As if she heard, Amy opened her eyes, and held out her arms. Neither said a word, but they hugged one another close, and everything was forgiven and forgotten.

Spring and then summer soon came on, and the lengthening of days gave long afternoons for work and play of all sorts. The girls included Laurie in much of their play, and one day he told them, "As a token of my gratitude, I have set up a post office in the lower corner of the garden. Letters, manuscripts, books and bundles can be passed there, and it will be uncommonly nice, I fancy."

His idea was greeted with great applause, and once set up, the P.O. flourished wonderfully. Nearly as many queer things passed through it as through the real office. Even the old gentleman liked the fun, and amused himself by sending odd bundles, mysterious messages and funny telegrams.

Beth was postmistress, for, being most at home, she could attend to it regularly, and dearly liked the daily task of unlocking the little door and distributing the mail. One July day she came in with her hands full, and went about the house leaving letters and parcels.

"Here's your posy, Mother! Laurie never forgets that," she said, putting a fresh nosegay in the vase that stood in "Marmee's corner," and was kept supplied by the affectionate boy.

"Miss Meg March, one letter and a glove," continued Beth, delivering the article to her sister, who sat near her mother, stitching wristbands.

"Why, I left a pair over there, and here is only one," said Meg, looking at the gray cotton glove. "Didn't you drop the other in the garden?"

"No, I'm sure I didn't; for there was one in the post office."

"I hate to have odd gloves! Never mind, the other may be found. My letter is only a translation of the German song I wanted; I think Mr. Brooke did it, for this isn't Laurie's writing."

"One letter for Jo, a book, and a funny old hat," said Beth, laughing, as she went into the study, where Jo sat writing.

"What a sly fellow Laurie is! I said I wished bigger hats were the fashion, because I burn my face every hot day. He said, 'Why mind the fashion? Wear a big hat and be comfortable.' I said I would if I had one, and he has sent me this to try me. I'll wear it, for fun, and show I don't care for the fashion." And hanging the hat on a bust of a Greek philosopher, Jo read her letter.

In a big, dashing hand, Laurie wrote:

DEAR JO,

What ho!

Some English girls and boys are coming to see me tomorrow, and I want to have a jolly time. If it's fine, I'm going to pitch my tent in Longmeadow, and row up the whole crew to lunch and croquet. They are nice people, and like such things. Brooke will go, to keep us boys steady, and Kate Vaughn will watch the girls. I want you all to come. Don't bother about food—I'll see to that, and everything else—only do come.

In a tearing hurry,

Yours ever, LAURIE.

Jo flew off to tell the news to Meg and Marmee. "Of course we can go, Mother? It will be such a help to Laurie, for I can row, and Meg see to lunch, and the children be useful in some way."

Mother approved their plan.

The next morning, when the sisters went out to meet Laurie's friends, they all looked their best, with happy faces under the hat brims.

Tents, lunch and croquet equipment had been sent on beforehand, and the two boats pushed off together, leaving Mr. Laurence waving his hat on shore. Laurie and Jo rowed one boat, Mr. Brooke and a boy named Ned the other, with pretty Meg sitting facing them. Mr. Brooke was a silent young man, with handsome brown eyes and a pleasant voice. Meg liked his quiet manners, and considered him a walking encyclopedia of useful knowledge. He never talked to her much, but he looked at her a good deal.

It was not far to Longmeadow. "Welcome to Camp Laurence!" said the young host, as they landed.

Frank, Beth, Amy and Grace sat down to watch the croquet game played by the other eight. Mr. Brooke chose Meg, Kate, the twenty-year-old chaperon, and Fred; Laurie chose Sallie, Jo and Ned. The Englishers played well, but the Americans played better.

Soon after, they had a very merry lunch, for everything seemed fresh and funny. Following lunch, they played party games and told stories.

Miss Kate in the meantime took out her sketchbook, and Meg watched her, while Mr. Brooke lay on the grass with a book, which he did not read.

"How beautifully you do it! I wish I could draw," said Meg.

"Why don't you learn? I should think you had taste and talent for it," replied Miss Kate.

Mr. Brooke lay on the grass.

"I haven't time. I'm a governess and must teach others."

"Oh, indeed!" said Miss Kate; but she might as well have said, "Dear me, how dreadful!" for her tone implied it.

Mr. Brooke looked up and said quickly, "Young ladies in America love independence as much as their ancestors did, and are admired and respected for supporting themselves."

"Oh, yes; of course it's very nice and proper in them to do so," said Miss Kate.

Meg was blushing, her feelings hurt by the superiority of Miss Kate's tone.

Mr. Brooke, breaking an awkward pause, asked, "Did the German song suit you, Miss March?"

"Oh, yes; it was very sweet, and I'm much obliged to whoever translated it for me."

At this, Miss Kate got up to look after Grace, leaving Mr. Brooke and Meg together.

"I forgot that English people rather turn up their noses at governesses, and don't treat them as we do," said Meg.

"Tutors also have rather a hard time of it there. There's no place like America for us workers, Miss Margaret," said Mr. Brooke.

"I'm glad I live in it then. I don't like my work, but I get a good deal of satisfaction out of it after all, so I won't complain; I only wish I liked teaching as you do."

"I think you would if you had Laurie for a pupil. I shall be very sorry to lose him next year," said Mr. Brooke.

"Going to college, I suppose?" Meg's lips asked that question, but her eyes added, "And what becomes of you?"

"Yes, it's high time he went, for he is ready; and as soon as he is off I shall turn soldier. I am needed."

"I am glad of that!" exclaimed Meg. "I should think every young man would want to go, though it is hard for the mothers and sisters who stay at home."

"I have neither, and very few friends to care whether I live or die," said Mr. Brooke.

"Laurie and his grandfather would care a great deal, and we should all be very sorry to have any harm happen to you," said Meg.

"Thank you; that sounds pleasant," said Mr. Brooke. Before he could say more, Ned, mounted on an old horse, came lumbering up, and there was no more quiet that day.

At sunset the tent was taken down, hampers packed, wickets pulled up, boats loaded, and the whole party floated down the river, singing at the tops of their voices.

Chapter 6

Castles in the Air

LAURIE LAY swinging to and fro in his hammock one warm September afternoon, wondering what his neighbors were doing, but too lazy to go and find out. Staring up into the green gloom of the chestnut trees above him, he dreamed dreams of all sorts, and was imagining himself tossing on the ocean in a voyage round the world, when the sound of voices brought him ashore in a flash. Peeping through the meshes of his hammock, he saw the Marches coming out, as if bound on some expedition.

"What in the world are those girls about now?" thought Laurie. Each wore a large, flapping hat, a brown linen pouch slung over one shoulder, and carried a long staff. Meg had a cushion, Jo a book, Beth a basket and Amy a portfolio. All walked quietly through the garden, out at the little back gate, and began to climb the hill that lay between the house and the river.

"Well!" said Laurie to himself. "To have a picnic and never ask me! They can't be going in the boat, for they haven't got the key. Perhaps they forgot it; I'll take it to them, and see what's going on."

The girls were quite out of sight by the time he leaped the fence and ran after them. Taking the shortest way to the boathouse, he waited for them to appear; but no one came, and he went up the hill to take a look. A group of pines covered one part of the hill, and from the heart of this green spot came the sound of their voices.

Laurie went and peeped through the greenery and saw the sisters sitting together in a shady nook, with sun and shadow flickering over them, the wind lifting their hair and cooling their hot faces. Meg sat on a cushion, sewing with her white hands, and looking as fresh and sweet as a rose, in her pink dress among the green. Beth was sorting the pinecones that lay thick under the hemlock near by, for she made pretty things of them. Amy was sketching a group of ferns, and Jo was knitting

This quiet party seemed most attractive.

as she read aloud. The boy felt that he ought to go away, because he was uninvited, yet he stayed, because home seemed very lonely, and this quiet party in the woods seemed most attractive to his restless spirit.

Beth looked up and saw him, and beckoned him with a smile.

"May I come in, please? Or shall I be a bother?" he asked.

Jo answered, "Of course you may. We should have asked you before, only we thought you wouldn't care for such a girl's game as this."

"I always liked your games; but if Meg doesn't want me, I'll go away."

"I've no objection, if you do something; it's against the rules to be idle here," replied Meg.

"Much obliged; I'll do anything if you'll let me stay a bit, for it's as dull as the Desert of Sahara down there. Shall I read, sew, draw, or do all at once?"

"Finish this story while I set my heel," said Jo, handing him the book.

"Yes'm," was the answer, as he began, doing his best to prove his gratitude for the favor of an admission into the "Busy Bee Society."

The story was not a long one and, when it was finished, he asked a few questions.

"Please, ma'am, could I inquire if this highly instructive and charming institution is a new one?"

"We have been going on with it all winter and summer," said Jo. "We have tried not to waste our holiday, but each has had a task, and worked at it with a will. The vacation is nearly over, and we are ever so glad that we didn't dawdle."

"Yes, I should think so," said Laurie, as he thought regretfully of his own idle ways.

"Mother likes to have us out of doors as much as possible, so we bring our work here and have nice times. From this hill we can look far away and see the country where we hope to live some time."

Jo pointed, and Laurie sat up to look, for through an opening in the wood one could see across the wide blue river, the meadows on the other side, far over the outskirts of the great city, to the green hills that rose to meet the sky. The sun was low, and the heavens glowed. Gold and purple clouds lay on the hilltops, and rising high into the light were silvery white peaks that shone like the towers of some Celestial City.

"How beautiful that is!" said Laurie.

"Jo talks about the country where we hope to live some time—the real country, she means, with pigs and chickens and haymaking. It would be nice, but I wish the beautiful country there in the sky was real, and we could go to it," said Beth.

"Wouldn't it be fun if all the castles in the air which we make could come true, and we could live in them?" said Jo.

"I've made such a number, it would be hard to choose which I'd have," said Laurie.

"You'd have to take your favorite one. What is it?" asked Meg.

"If I tell mine, will you tell yours?"

"Yes, if the girls will too."

"We will. Now, Laurie."

"After I'd seen as much of the world as I want to, I'd like to settle in Germany, and have just as much music as I choose. I'm to be a famous musician myself, and all creation is to rush to hear me; and I'm never to be bothered about money or business, but just enjoy myself, and live for what I like. That's my favorite castle. What's yours, Meg?"

Margaret seemed to find it a little hard to tell hers, but finally said, "I should like a lovely house, full of all sorts of luxurious things—nice food, pretty clothes, handsome furniture, pleasant people and heaps of money. I am to be mistress of it, and manage it as I like, with plenty of servants, so I never need work a bit. How I should enjoy it! For I wouldn't be idle, but do good and make everyone love me dearly."

"Why don't you say you'd have a splendid, wise, good husband, and some angelic little children? You know your castle wouldn't be perfect without them," said Jo.

"You'd have nothing but horses, inkstands and novels in yours," said Meg.

"Wouldn't I, though? I'd have a stable full of Arabian horses, rooms piled with books, and I'd write out of a magic inkstand, so that my works should be as famous as Laurie's music. I want to do something splendid before I go into my castle—something heroic or wonderful, that won't be forgotten after I'm dead. I think I shall write books, and get rich and famous: that would suit me, so that is *my* favorite dream."

"Mine is to stay at home safe with Father and Mother, and help take care of the family," said Beth.

"Don't you wish for anything else?" asked Laurie.

"Since I had my little piano, I am perfectly satisfied. I only wish we may all keep well and be together; nothing else."

"I have ever so many wishes, but the pet one is to be an artist, and go to Rome, and do fine pictures, and be the best artist in the whole world," said Amy.

"We're an ambitious set, aren't we? Every one of us, but Beth, wants to be rich and famous, and gorgeous in every respect. I do wonder if any of us will ever get our wishes," said Laurie.

"I've got the key to my castle in the air, but whether I can unlock the door remains to be seen," said Jo.

"I've got the key to mine, but I'm not allowed to try it. Hang college!" muttered Laurie.

"Here's mine!" and Amy waved her pencil.

"I haven't got any," said Meg.

"Yes, you have," said Laurie.

"Where?"

"In your face."

"Nonsense; that's of no use."

"Wait and see if it doesn't bring you something worth having," replied the boy.

"If we are alive ten years from now," said Jo, "let's meet, and see how many of us have got our wishes, or how much nearer we are than now."

"I hope I shall have done something to be proud of by that time, but I'm such a lazy dog, I'm afraid I shall dawdle, Jo," said Laurie.

"You need a motive, Mother says; and when you get it, she is sure you'll work splendidly."

"Is she? By Jupiter! I will, if I only get the chance!" cried Laurie. "I ought to be satisfied to please Grandfather, and I do try, but it's working against the grain, you see, and comes hard. He want me to be an India merchant, as he was, and I'd rather be shot. I hate tea and silk and spices, and every sort of rubbish his old ships bring, and I don't care how soon they go to the bottom when I own them. Going to college ought to satisfy him, for if I give him four years he ought to let me off from business; but he's set, and I've got to do just as he did, unless I break away and please myself, as my father did. If there was anyone left to stay with the old gentleman, I'd do it tomorrow."

"I advise you to sail away in one of your ships, and never come home again till you have tried your own way," said Jo.

"That's not right, Jo; you mustn't talk in that way, and Laurie mustn't take your bad advice. You should do just what your grandfather wishes, my dear boy," said Meg. "Do your best at college, and when he sees that you try to please him, I'm sure he won't be hard or unjust to you. Do your duty, and you'll get your reward."

That night, when Beth played piano for Mr. Laurence, Laurie, standing in the shadow of a curtain, listened to the little charmer, whose simple music always quieted the old man, who sat with his head in his hands, thinking of the dead child he had loved so much. Remembering the conversation of the afternoon, the boy said to himself, "I'll let my castle go, and stay with the dear old gentleman while he needs me, for I am all he has."

Chapter 7

Secrets

J O WAS very busy in the attic, for the October days began to grow chilly, and the afternoons were short. For two or three hours the sun lay warmly in the high window, showing Jo seated on the old sofa, writing busily, with her papers spread out upon a trunk before her, while Scrabble, the pet rat, walked the beams overhead. Jo scribbled away till the last page was filled, when she signed her name and threw down her pen, exclaiming:

"There, I've done my best! If this won't suit, I shall have to wait till I can do better."

Lying back on the sofa, she read the manuscript through; then she tied it up with red ribbon, and sat a minute looking at it. Jo pulled out another set of papers from her desk and, putting both in her pocket, crept downstairs.

She put on her hat and jacket and, going to the back entry window, got out upon the roof of a low porch, swung herself down to the grassy bank, and took a roundabout way to the road. Once there, she hailed a passing public coach, and rolled away to town.

If anyone had been watching her he would have thought her movements strange, for, on getting out of the coach, she went off in a hurry till she reached a certain number in a certain busy street. She went into the doorway, looked up the stairs, pulled her hat over her eyes, and walked up the stairs.

In ten minutes Jo came running downstairs with a very red face. Laurie, idling his time away in a billiards hall across the street, happened to see her leave the building, and he came out and approached her.

She took a roundabout way to the road.

"What are you up to, Jo?" he asked.

"What were you doing, sir?"

"I have billiards at home, but it's no fun unless you have good players; so, as I'm fond of it, I come sometimes and have a game with Ned Moffat or some of the other fellows."

"Oh, dear, I'm so sorry, for you'll get to liking it better and better, and will waste time and money, and grow like those dreadful boys. I did hope you'd stay respectable and be a satisfaction to your friends," said Jo.

"I like harmless fun now and then, don't you?"

"But don't get wild, will you?"

Laurie walked in silence for a few minutes, and Jo watched him, wishing she had held her tongue, for his eyes looked angry.

"Are you going to deliver lectures all the way home?" he asked. "Because if you are, I'll go another way; if you are not, I'd like to walk with you and tell you something very interesting."

"I won't preach any more, and I'd like to hear the news."

"It's a secret, and if I tell you, you must tell me yours."

"You won't tease me in private?"

"I never tease," said Laurie.

"Well," said Jo, "I've left two stories with a newspaper man, and he's to give his answer next week."

"Hurrah for Miss March, the famous American authoress!" cried Laurie.

"Hush! It won't come to anything, I dare say; but I couldn't rest till I had tried, and I said nothing about it, because I didn't want anyone else to be disappointed."

"It won't fail. Won't it be fun to see them in print?"

Jo was pleased with the thought, but said, "What's *your* secret? Play fair."

"I may get into trouble for telling, but I didn't promise not to, so I will. I know where Meg's glove is."

"Is that all?" said Jo.

He whispered a few words in Jo's ear.

She said, "How do you know?"

"Saw it."

"Where?"

"In his pocket."

"All this time?"

"Yes; isn't that romantic?"

"No, it's horrid."

"Don't you like it?"

"Of course I don't. It's ridiculous; it won't be allowed. The idea of anybody coming to take Meg away! No, thank you." Lately she had felt that Margaret was fast getting to be a woman, and Laurie's secret made her dread the separation which must surely come sometime, and now seemed very near.

For the next week or two Jo behaved so strangely that her sisters wondered about her. She rushed to the door when the postman rang, was rude to Mr. Brooke whenever they met, would sit looking at Meg with a sad face, and Laurie and she were always making signs to one another until the girls declared they had both lost their wits. On the second Saturday after Jo got out of the window, Meg, as she sat sewing at her window, was scandalized by the sight of Laurie chasing Jo all over the garden and finally capturing her in Amy's bower. What went on there, Meg could not see, but shrieks of laughter were heard, followed by the murmur of voices and a great flapping of newspapers.

Jo lay on the sofa and pretended to read.

"What shall we do with that girl? She never will behave like a young lady," sighed Meg.

"I hope she won't; she is so funny and dear as she is," said Beth.

"It's very difficult, but we can never make her as she should be," added Amy.

In a few minutes Jo bounced in, laid herself on the sofa, and pretended to read.

"Have you anything interesting there?" asked Meg.

"Nothing but a story; won't amount to much, I guess," returned Jo.

"You'd better read it aloud; that will amuse us and keep you out of mischief," said Amy.

"What's the name of the story?" asked Beth.

"'The Rival Painters.'"

"That sounds well; read it," said Meg.

With a loud "Hem!" and a long breath, Jo began to read very fast. The girls listened with interest, for the tale was romantic.

"Who wrote it?" asked Beth.

The reader suddenly sat up, cast away the paper, and replied, "Your sister."

"You?" cried Meg.

"It's very good," said Amy.

"I knew it! I knew it! Oh, my Jo, I am so proud!" and Beth began to hug her sister.

How delighted they all were! How Meg wouldn't believe it till she saw the words "Miss Josephine March" actually printed in the paper; how proud Mrs. March was when she knew it; how Jo laughed, with tears in her eyes; and how the newspaper passed from hand to hand.

"Tell us all about it." "When did it come?" "How much did you get for it?" "What will Father say?" cried the family, all in one breath, as they clustered about Jo.

"Stop jabbering, girls, and I'll tell you everything," said the author. Having told how she submitted her stories, Jo added, "And when I went to get my answer, the man said he liked them both, but didn't pay beginners, only let them print in his paper. So I let him have the two stories, and today this was sent to me, and Laurie caught me with it and insisted on seeing it, so I let him; and he said it was good, and I shall write more, and he's going to get the next paid for, and I *am* so happy, for in time I may be able to support myself and help the girls."

Jo's breath gave out here. To be independent and earn the praise of those she loved were the dearest wishes of her heart, and this seemed to be the first step towards that happy end.

Chapter 8

A Telegram

NOVEMBER IS the most disagreeable month in the whole year," said Margaret, standing at the window one dull afternoon, looking out at the frostbitten garden.

Beth, who sat at the other window, said, smiling, "If something very pleasant should happen now to this family, we should think it a delightful month. And look, two pleasant things are going to happen right away. Marmee is coming down the street, and Laurie is tramping through the garden as if he had something nice to tell."

In they both came, Mrs. March with her usual question, "Any letter from Father, girls?" and Laurie with, "Won't some of you come for a drive?"

All the girls but Meg agreed to come along.

"Can I do anything for you, Madam Mother?" asked Laurie.

"No, thank you, except call at the post office, if you'll be so kind, dear. It's our day for a letter, and the postman hasn't been. Father is as regular as the sun, but there's some delay on the way, perhaps."

A ring at the door interrupted her, and a minute after Hannah came in with a letter.

"It's one of them horrid telegraph things, mum," she said, handing it over.

At the word "telegraph" Mrs. March snatched it, read the two lines it contained, and dropped back into her chair. Jo now took it and read aloud, in a frightened voice:

"Mrs. March:
  Your husband is very ill. Come at once.
        S. Hale,
      Blank Hospital, Washington."

How suddenly the world seemed to change, as the girls gathered about their mother, feeling as if all the happiness and support of their lives was about to be taken from them. Mrs. March read the message over, and stretched out her arms to her daughters, saying, in a tone they never forgot, "I shall go at once, but it may be too late. Oh, children, children, help me to bear it!"

Mrs. March stretched out her arms to her daughters.

For several minutes there was nothing but the sound of sobbing in the room, mingled with words of comfort and hopeful whispers. Poor Hannah was the first to recover; with her, work was the cure for most hurts.

"The Lord keep the dear man! I won't waste no time a-cryin', but git your things ready right away, mum," she said, as she wiped her face on her apron, gave her mistress a warm shake of the hand, and went away, to work like three women in one.

"She's right; there's no time for tears now. Be calm, girls, and let me think."

In a few moments she asked, "Where's Laurie?"

"Here, ma'am. Oh, let me do something!" cried the boy, hurrying from the next room.

"Send a telegram saying I will come at once. The next train goes early in the morning. I'll take that."

"What else? The horses are ready," he said.

"Leave a note at Aunt March's." She sat down and wrote the note, for the money for the sad little journey would have to be borrowed. "Now go, dear, but don't drive at a desperate pace; there is no need of that."

And off Laurie went.

"Jo, run to the rooms, and tell Mrs. King that I can't come. On the way get these things. I'll write them down; they'll be needed, and I must go prepared for nursing. Hospital supplies are not always plentiful. Beth, go and ask Mr. Laurence for a couple of bottles of old wine: I'm not too proud to beg for Father, he shall have the best of everything. Amy, tell Hannah to get down the black trunk; and, Meg, come and help me find my things."

Everyone scattered like leaves before a gust of wind.

Mr. Laurence came hurrying back with Beth, bringing every comfort the kind old gentleman could think of for Mr. March, and promises of protection for the girls during their mother's absence. There was nothing he didn't offer, even himself as an escort to Mrs. March. But she would not hear of the old gentleman's undertaking the long journey. He left, saying he would be back soon.

In a short while, Mr. Brooke came over, and Meg discovered him in the entry.

"I'm very sorry to hear of this, Miss March," he said. "I came to offer myself as escort to your mother. Mr. Laurence has work for me in Washington, and it will give me real satisfaction to be of service to her there."

Meg put out her hand, with a face full of gratitude. "How kind you are! Mother will accept, I'm sure, and it will be such a relief to know that she has someone to take care of her. Thank you very, very much!"

She led him into the parlor, saying she would call her mother.

Everything was arranged by the time Laurie returned, with a note from Aunt March enclosing the desired money. Mrs. March put the money in her purse, and went on with her preparations.

The short afternoon wore away; all the other errands were done, but still Jo did not return home from Mrs. King's. They began to get anxious, but finally she came walking in with a very strange expression on her face, as she laid a roll of bills before her mother, saying, "That's my contribution towards making Father comfortable, and bringing him home!"

"My dear, where did you get it? Twenty-five dollars? Jo, I hope you haven't done anything rash?"

"No, it's mine honestly; I didn't beg, borrow, or steal it. I earned it; and I don't think you'll blame me, for I only sold what was my own."

As she spoke, Jo took off her bonnet, and a general outcry arose, for all her long, thick hair was cut short.

"Your hair! Your beautiful hair!"

As everyone exclaimed, Jo said, rumpling up the little hair left on her head, "It doesn't affect the fate of the nation, so don't cry, Beth. It will do my brains good to have that mop taken off; my head feels light and cool. I'm satisfied, so please take the money, and let's have supper."

"Tell me all about it, Jo. I am not quite satisfied, but I can't blame you, for I know how willingly you sacrificed it. But, my dear, it was not necessary, and I'm afraid you will regret it one of these days," said Mrs. March.

"No, I won't!" returned Jo. "I was wanting to do something for Father. I hadn't the least idea of selling my hair at first, but as I went along I kept thinking what I could do. In a barber's window I saw tails of hair with the price marked, and one black tail, not so thick as mine, was forty dollars. It came over me all of a sudden that I had one thing to make money out of, and without stopping to think, I walked in, asked if they bought hair, and what they would give for mine.

All her long, thick hair was cut short.

"The barber rather stared at first, as if he wasn't used to having girls bounce into his shop and ask him to buy their hair. He said he didn't care about mine, it wasn't the fashionable color. Then I told him why I needed the money, and it changed his mind. His wife overheard my story to him, and she said so kindly, 'Take it, Thomas. I'd do as much for our son any day if I had hair worth selling.' I took a last look at my hair while the man got his things, and that was the end of it. I will confess, though, I felt odd when I saw the dear old hair laid out on the table, and felt only the short, rough ends on my head. The woman saw me look at it, and picked out a long lock for me to keep. I'll give it to you, Marmee, just to remember."

Mrs. March took the wavy brown lock and laid it away in her desk. She said, "Thank you, deary."

No one wanted to go to bed when at ten o'clock Mrs. March put by the last finished job, and said, "Come, girls." Beth went to the piano and played the father's favorite hymn; all began bravely, but broke down one by one, till Beth was left alone, singing with all her heart.

"Go to bed, and don't talk, for we must be up early and shall need all the sleep we can get. Good night, my darlings," said Mrs. March, as the hymn ended.

They kissed her quietly, and went to bed. Beth and Amy soon fell asleep in spite of the great troubles, but Meg lay awake, thinking the most serious thoughts she had ever known in her short life. Jo lay motionless, and seemed asleep, till a stifled sob came from her.

"Jo, dear, what is it? Are you crying about Father?"

"No, not now. My hair!" burst out poor Jo.

Meg kissed and petted her sister.

"I'm not sorry," said Jo. "I'd do it again tomorrow, if I could. Don't tell anyone, it's all over now. I thought you were asleep, so I just made a little private moan for my one beauty."

In the cold gray dawn the sisters lit their lamp; as they dressed, they agreed to say good-by cheerfully and send their mother on her journey unsaddened by tears or complaints from them. Everything seemed very strange when they went down—so dim and still outside, so full of light and bustle within. The big trunk stood ready in the hall, Mother's cloak and bonnet lay on the sofa, and Mother herself sat trying to eat, but looking so pale and worn that the girls found it very hard to keep their resolution. Meg's eyes kept filling in spite of herself, Jo had to hide her face more than once, and the little girls wore a troubled expression, as if sorrow was a new experience to them.

Nobody talked much, but as the time drew near, and they sat waiting for the carriage, Mrs. March said to the girls, who were all busied about her:

"Children, I leave you to Hannah's care and Mr. Laurence's protection. Hannah is faithfulness itself, and our good neighbor will guard you as if you were his own. I have no fears for you. Don't grieve and fret when I am gone. Go on with your work as usual, for work is a blessed comfort. Hope and keep busy."

"Yes, Mother."

"Meg, dear, be prudent, watch over your sisters, consult Hannah, and, in any trouble, go to Mr. Laurence. Be patient, Jo, don't get too sad or do rash things; write to me often, and be my brave girl, ready to help and cheer us all. Beth, comfort yourself with your music, and be faithful to the little home duties; and you, Amy, help all you can, be obedient, and keep happy safe at home."

"We will, Mother! We will!"

"Good-by, my darlings! God bless and keep us all!" whispered Mrs. March, as she kissed one dear little face after the other, and hurried into the carriage.

Then Laurie and his grandfather came over to see her off.

As she rolled away with Mr. Brooke, the sun came out, and, looking back, she saw it shining on the group at the gate. They smiled and waved their hands; and the last thing she saw as she turned the corner, was the four bright faces, and behind them, like a bodyguard, old Mr. Laurence, faithful Hannah and devoted Laurie.

Chapter 9

Little Faithful

M EG, I wish you'd go and see the Hummels; you know Mother told us not to forget them," said Beth, ten days after Mrs. March's departure.

"I'm too tired to go this afternoon," replied Meg, as she sewed.

"Can't you, Jo?" asked Beth.

"Too stormy for me with my cold."

"I thought it was almost well."

"It's well enough for me to go out with Laurie, but not well enough to go to the Hummels'," said Jo.

"Why don't you go yourself?" asked Meg.

"I *have* been every day, but the baby is sick, and I don't know what to do for it. Mrs. Hummel goes away to work, and her daughter takes care of it; but it gets sicker and sicker, and I think you or Hannah ought to go."

Meg promised she would go tomorrow.

"Ask Hannah for some nice little basket of food, and take it round, Beth; the air will do you good," said Jo. "I'd go, but I want to finish my writing."

"My head aches, and I'm tired, so I thought maybe one of you would go," said Beth.

"Amy will be in soon, and she will run down for us," suggested Meg.

"Well, I'll rest a little and wait for her."

So Beth lay down on the sofa, and the others returned to their work, and the Hummels were forgotten. An hour passed: Amy did not come, Meg went to her room to try on a new dress, Jo was absorbed in her story, and Hannah was sound asleep before the kitchen fire, when Beth quietly put on her hood, filled her basket with odds and ends for the poor children, and went out into the chilly air. It was late when she came back, and no one saw her creep upstairs and shut herself into her mother's room. Half an hour after, Jo went to "Mother's closet" for something, and there found Beth sitting looking very sad, with red eyes, and a medicine bottle in her hand.

"What's the matter?" cried Jo.

"What's the matter?" cried Jo.

Beth put out her hand as if to warn her off, and asked, "You've had the scarlet fever, haven't you?"

"Years ago, when Meg did. Why?"

"Then I'll tell you. Oh, Jo, the baby's dead!"

"What baby?"

"Mrs. Hummel's; it died in my lap before she got home," cried Beth, with a sob.

"My poor dear, how dreadful for you! I ought to have gone," said Jo, taking her sister in her arms as she sat down in her mother's big chair.

"It wasn't dreadful, Jo, only so sad! I saw in a minute that it was sicker, but Lotte said her mother had gone for a doctor, so I took Baby and let Lotte rest. It seemed asleep, but all of a sudden it gave a little cry and trembled, and then lay very still. I tried to warm its feet, and Lotte gave it some milk, but it didn't stir, and I knew it was dead."

"Don't cry, dear! What did you do?"

"I just sat and held it softly till Mrs. Hummel came with the doctor. He said it was dead, and looked at the other two children, who have got sore throats. 'Scarlet fever, ma'am. Ought to have called me before,' he said. Mrs. Hummel told him she was poor, and had tried to cure the baby herself, but now it was too late, and she could only ask him to help the others. It was very sad, and I cried with them till he turned round, all of a sudden, and told me to go home and take belladonna right away, or I'd have the fever."

"No, you won't!" cried Jo, hugging her close, with a frightened look. "Oh, Beth, if you should be sick I never could forgive myself! What shall we do?"

"Don't be frightened, I guess I shan't have it badly. I looked in Mother's book, and saw that it begins with headache, sore throat, and strange feelings like mine, so I did take some belladonna, and I feel better," said Beth.

"If Mother was only at home!" exclaimed Jo. "You've been over the baby for more than a week, and among the others who are going to have it; so I'm afraid you *are* going to have it, Beth. I'll call Hannah, she knows all about sickness."

"Don't let Amy come; she never had it, and I should hate to give it to her. Can't you and Meg have it over again?"

"I guess not; don't care if I do; serve me right, selfish pig, to let you go, and stay writing rubbish myself!" muttered Jo, as she went to consult Hannah.

There was no need to worry, Hannah assured Jo; everyone had scarlet fever, and, if rightly treated, nobody died—all of which Jo believed.

"Now I'll tell you what we'll do," said Hannah, when she had examined and questioned Beth, "we will have Dr. Bangs take a look at you, dear, and see that we start right; then we'll send Amy off to Aunt March's for a spell, to keep her out of harm's way, and one of you girls can stay at home and amuse Beth for a day or two."

Beth chose Jo to be with her, which left Meg feeling a little hurt, yet rather relieved on the whole, for she did not like nursing, and Jo did. "I'll go tell Amy," said Meg.

Amy rebelled, and declared that she had rather have the fever than go to Aunt March. Meg reasoned, pleaded, commanded. Amy protested that she would *not* go; and Meg left her to ask Hannah what should be done. Before she came back, Laurie walked into the parlor to find Amy sobbing, with her head in the sofa cushions. She told her story, expecting to be consoled, but Laurie only put his hands in his pockets and walked about the room, whistling softly, as he knit his brows in deep thought. Soon he sat down beside her and said, "Now, be a sensible little woman, and do as they say. No, don't cry, but hear what a jolly plan I've got. You go to Aunt March's, and I'll come and take you out every day driving or walking, and we'll have capital times."

"I don't wish to be sent off as if I was in the way," began Amy.

"Bless your heart, child, it's to keep you well. You don't want to be sick, do you?"

"No, I'm sure I don't; but I dare say I shall be, for I've been with Beth all the time."

"That's the very reason you ought to go away at once, so that you may escape it. Change of air will keep you well; or, if it does not entirely, you will have the fever more lightly. I advise you to be off as soon as you can, for scarlet fever is no joke, Miss."

"But it's dull at Aunt March's, and she is so cross," said Amy.

"It won't be dull with me popping in every day to tell you how Beth is, and take you out. The old lady likes me, so she won't peck at us, whatever we do."

"Well—I guess—I will," said Amy.

"Good girl! Call Meg, and tell her you'll give in," said Laurie.

Meg and Jo came down and heard Amy's statement, and were surprised but pleased.

Laurie asked them, "Shall I telegraph to your mother or do anything?"

"That is what troubles me," said Meg. "I think we ought to tell her if Beth is really ill, but Hannah says we mustn't, for Mother can't leave Father, and it will only make them anxious. Beth won't be sick long, and Hannah knows just what to do, and Mother said we were to mind her, so I suppose we must, but it doesn't seem quite right to me."

Laurie went off to fetch Dr. Bangs. He said Beth had symptoms of the fever, but thought she would have it lightly. Amy was ordered off at once, and she departed with Jo and Laurie as her escorts.

Aunt March received them with her usual impatience.

"What do you want now?" she asked, looking over her spectacles, while her parrot, sitting on the back of her chair, called out:

"Go away. No boys allowed here."

Laurie went to the window, while Jo told the story.

In response, Aunt March said, "No more than I expected, if you are allowed to go poking about among poor folks. Amy can stay and make herself useful, if she isn't sick."

Beth did have the fever, and was much sicker than anyone but Hannah and the doctor suspected. The girls knew nothing about illness, and Mr. Laurence was not allowed to see her, so Hannah did everything all her own way, and busy Dr. Bangs did his best, but left a good deal to the excellent nurse. Meg stayed home, lest she should infect the Kings, and kept house, feeling a little guilty when she wrote letters in which no mention was made of Beth's illness. Jo devoted herself to Beth day and night. There came a time during the fever fits that Beth began to talk in a hoarse, broken voice, to play on the covers, as if on her beloved little piano, and try to sing with a swollen throat; a time when she did not know the familiar faces round her, but addressed them by wrong names, and called for her mother. Then Jo grew frightened, Meg begged to be allowed to write the truth, and even Hannah said she "would think of it, though there was no danger yet." A letter from Washington added to their trouble, for Mr. March had had a relapse, and could not think of coming home for a long while.

Beth lay hour after hour, tossing to and fro, with meaningless words on her lips, or sank into a heavy sleep which gave her no peace. Dr. Bangs came twice a day, Hannah sat up at night, Meg

Beth lay hour after hour, turning to and fro.

kept a telegram in her desk all ready to send off at any minute, and Jo never stirred from Beth's side.

The first of December was a wintry day, for a bitter wind blew, and snow fell fast. When Dr. Bangs came that morning, he looked long at Beth, held her hot hand in both his own a minute, and laid it gently down, saying to Hannah: "If Mrs. March can leave her husband, she'd better be sent for."

Hannah nodded without speaking, Meg dropped down into a chair, and Jo ran to the parlor, snatched up the telegram, and, throwing on her things, rushed out into the storm. She was soon back, and, while taking off her coat, Laurie came in with a letter, saying that Mr. March was getting better again. Jo read it, but the heavy weight did not seem lifted off her heart, and Laurie asked, "What is it? Is Beth worse?"

"I've sent for Mother," she said. "The doctor told us to."

"Oh, Jo, it's not so bad as that?" cried Laurie.

"Yes, it is; she doesn't know us, she doesn't look like my Beth, and there's nobody to help us bear it, with Mother and Father both gone."

As the tears streamed down poor Jo's cheeks, she stretched out her hand in a helpless sort of way, and Laurie took it in his, whispering: "I'm here. Hold on to me, Jo, dear!"

She could not speak, but she did "hold on," and the warm grasp of the friendly hand comforted her sore heart. Laurie wanted to say something tender and comforting, but no fitting words came to him, so he stood silent, gently stroking her bent head as her mother used to do. Soon she dried the tears which had relieved her, and looked up.

"Thank you, Laurie, I'm better now; I don't feel so forlorn, and will try to bear it if it comes."

She shed tears now, and Laurie drew his hand across his eyes, having a choking feeling in his throat. As Jo's sobs quieted, Laurie said, "I don't think she will die; she's so good, and we all love her so much, I don't believe God will take her away yet."

"The good and dear people always do die," groaned Jo.

"Poor girl, you're worn out. It isn't like you to be like this. Tonight I'll give you something that will warm your heart," said Laurie.

"What is it?" cried Jo.

"I telegraphed to your mother yesterday, and Brooke answered she'd come at once, and she'll be here tonight, and everything will be all right."

"Oh, Laurie! Oh, Mother! I am so glad!"

"Grandpa said it was high time we did something, and so he sent me off to the telegraph office yesterday. The late train is in at 2 A.M., and I shall go to pick your mother up, and you've only got to keep Beth safe till that blessed lady gets here."

"Laurie, you're an angel! How shall I ever thank you? Bless you, bless you!"

When Jo went upstairs and told the news, Hannah said, "That's the interferingest chap I ever see, but I forgive him and do hope Mrs. March is coming on right away."

A breath of fresh air seemed to blow through the house. Everything appeared to feel the hopeful change; Beth's bird began to chirp again, and a half-bloomed rose was discovered on Amy's bush in the window; every time Jo and Meg met, their faces broke into smiles as they hugged one another, whispering, "Mother's coming, dear! Mother's coming!" Everyone rejoiced but Beth; she lay in a heavy stupor, her face vacant, her once busy hands weak and wasted, her hair scattered rough and tangled on the pillow. All day she lay so, only rousing now and then to mutter, "Water!" All day Jo and Meg hovered over her, watching, waiting, hoping and trusting in God and Mother; and all day the snow fell, the bitter wind raged, and the hours dragged slowly by. But night came at last, and every time the clock struck, the sisters, still sitting on either side of the bed, looked at each other with brightening eyes, for each hour brought help nearer. The doctor had been in to say that some change, for better or worse, would probably take place about midnight, at which time he would return.

The girls never forgot that night, for no sleep came to them as they kept their watch, with that dreadful sense of powerlessness which comes to us in hours like these.

"I wish I had no heart, it aches so," sighed Meg.

"If life is often as hard as this, I don't see how we ever shall get through it," added Jo.

Here the clock struck twelve, and both forgot themselves in watching Beth, for they saw a change pass over her pale face. The house was still as death, and nothing but the wailing of the wind broke the deep hush. Weary Hannah slept on, and no one but the sisters saw the shadow which seemed to fall upon the little bed. An hour went by, and nothing happened except Laurie's quiet departure for the station. Another hour—still no one came, and anxious fears of delay in the storm, or accidents by the way, or, worst of all, a great trouble at Washington, haunted the poor girls.

It was past two, when Jo, who stood at the window, heard a movement by the bed, and, turning quickly, saw Meg kneeling before her mother's easy chair with her face hidden. A fear passed coldly over Jo, as she thought, "Beth is dead, and Meg is afraid to tell me."

She was back in her post in an instant, and to her excited eyes a great change seemed to have taken place. The look of

Jo whispered, "Good-by, my Beth; good-by!"

pain was gone, and the beloved little face looked so pale and peaceful, that Jo leaned over this dearest of her sisters, and kissed the damp forehead, and whispered, "Good-by, my Beth; good-by!"

As if waked by the stir, Hannah started out of her sleep, hurried to the bed, looked at Beth, felt her hands, listened at her lips, and then, throwing her apron over her head, sat down to rock to and fro, exclaiming, under her breath, "The fever's turned, she's sleeping natural, her skin's damp, and she breathes easy. Praise be given! Oh, my goodness me!"

Jo and Meg crept into the dark hall, and, sitting on the stairs, held each other close, rejoicing with hearts too full for words. When they came back to be kissed and cuddled by faithful Hannah, they found Beth lying, as she used to do, with her cheek on her hand, and breathing quietly, as if just fallen asleep.

"If Mother would only come now!" said Jo.

"See," said Meg, coming up with a white, half-opened rose, "I thought this would hardly be ready to lay in Beth's hand tomorrow if she—went away from us. But it has blossomed in the night, and now I mean to put it in my vase here, so that when the darling wakes, the first things she sees will be the little rose, and Mother's face."

Never had the sun risen so beautifully as it did to the heavy eyes of Meg and Jo, as they looked out in the early morning.

"It looks like a fairy world," said Meg, smiling to herself.

"Hark!" cried Jo.

Yes, there was a sound of bells at the door below, a cry from Hannah, and then Laurie's voice saying in a joyful whisper, "Girls, she's come! She's come!"

Chapter 10

Confidential

I DON'T think I have any words in which to tell the meeting of the mother and daughters; such hours are beautiful to live, but very hard to describe, so I will leave it to the imagination of my readers, merely saying that the house was full of genuine happiness. When Beth woke from that long, healing sleep, the first things she saw were the little rose and Mother's face. Too weak to wonder, she only smiled and nestled close into the loving arms about her. Then she slept again, and the girls waited upon their mother; for she would not let go of the thin hand which clung to hers even in sleep.

Hannah had "dished up" an astonishing breakfast for the traveler, and Meg and Jo fed their mother, while they listened to her whispered story of Father's state, Mr. Brooke's promise to stay and nurse him, the delays which the storm caused and the comfort Laurie had given her when she arrived, worn out.

What a strange yet pleasant day that was!

In the afternoon, after everyone had rested, Mrs. March went to see Amy at Aunt March's. Amy cried with joy upon seeing her mother, and was so happy as she sat in Mother's lap and told the story of her stay with her aunt.

When that time was over, Mrs. March said, "Now I must go back to Beth. Keep up your heart, little daughter, and we will soon have you home again." There was still the threat of the disease being passed to Amy.

That evening, while Meg was writing to Father, Jo slipped upstairs into Beth's room, and found her mother in her usual place.

"I want to tell you something, Mother."

"About Meg?"

"Yes, it's about her, and though it's a little thing, it bothers me. Last summer Meg left a pair of gloves over at the Laurences', and only one was returned. We forgot all about it, till Laurie told me that Mr. Brooke had it."

"Do you think Meg cares for him?"

"Mercy me! I don't know anything about love and such non-sense! I know you'll take his part, though; he's been good to

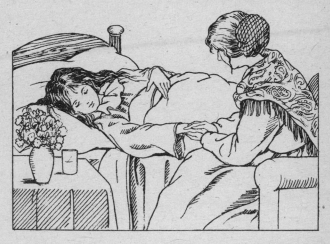

She would not let go of the thin hand which clung to hers.

Father, and you won't send him away, but let Meg marry him, if she wants to. Mean thing! To go helping Papa and you, just to get you into liking him."

"My dear, don't get angry about it, and I will tell you how it happened. John Brooke went with me at Mr. Laurence's request, and was so devoted to poor Father that we couldn't help getting fond of him. He was perfectly open about Meg, for he told us he loved her, but would earn a comfortable home before he asked her to marry him. He only wanted our permission to love her, and the right to make her love him if he could. He is a truly excellent young man, and we could not refuse to listen to him, but I will not consent to Meg engaging herself so young."

"Of course not; it would be idiotic! I just wish I could marry Meg myself, and keep her safe in the family. But now she'll go and fall in love, and there's the end of peace and fun, and cozy times together. I see it all! They'll go lovering around the house. Oh, dear me! Why weren't we all boys, then there wouldn't be any bother!"

"It is natural and right you should all go to homes of your own in time, Jo, but I do want to keep my girls as long as I can; and I am sorry that this happened so soon, for Meg is only seventeen, and it will be some years before John can make a home for her. If she and John love one another, they can wait until she is twenty, and test the love by doing so."

"Hadn't you rather have her marry a rich man?" asked Jo.

"Money is a good and useful thing, Jo. But I am not ambitious for a splendid fortune, a fine position, or a great name for my girls. I know, by experience, how much happiness can be had in a plain little house, where the daily bread is earned. I am content to see Meg begin humbly, for, if I am not mistaken, she will be rich in the possession of a good man's heart, and that is better than a fortune."

"I understand, Mother, but I'm disappointed about Meg, for I'd planned to have her marry Laurie by and by, and sit in the lap of luxury all her days. Wouldn't it be nice?" asked Jo.

"He is younger than she, you know," began Mrs. March.

"Only a little," interrupted Jo. "He's old for his age, and tall. He's rich and kind and good, and loves us all."

"I'm afraid Laurie is hardly grown-up enough for Meg. Don't make plans, Jo, but let time and their own hearts find each other."

Like sunshine after storm were the peaceful weeks which followed. Beth and Mr. March improved rapidly, and he talked of returning early in the new year. Beth was soon able to lie on the study sofa all day, amusing herself with the cats at first, and, in time, with dolls. Amy celebrated her return from Aunt March's by giving away as many of her treasures as she could get her sisters to accept.

Several days of unusually mild weather brought in a splendid Christmas Day. Hannah "felt in her bones" that it was going to be an unusually fine day. Mr. March wrote to say that he should soon be with them; Beth felt especially well that morning, and was carried to the window to behold the gift of Jo and Laurie. Like elves, they had worked by night and created a comical surprise. Out in the garden stood a snow maiden, crowned with holly, bearing a basket of fruit and flowers in one hand, a great roll of new music in the other, a colorful Afghan blanket, and a Christmas carol coming out of the snow maiden's lips, on a pink paper streamer.

How Beth laughed when she saw it, how Laurie ran up and down to bring in the gifts, and what silly speeches Jo made as she presented them!

"I'm so full of happiness, that, if Father was only here, I couldn't hold one drop more," said Beth, as Jo carried her off to the study to rest after the excitement.

Now and then, in this world, things do happen in storybook fashion. Half an hour after everyone had said they were so happy they could only hold one drop more, the drop came. Laurie opened the parlor door and popped his head in very quietly. He said, "Here's another Christmas present for the March family."

Before the words were out of his mouth, he was whisked away, and in his place appeared a tall man, muffled up to the eyes, leaning on the arm of another tall man, who tried to say something and couldn't. Of course, there was a general stampede, and for several minutes everybody seemed to lose their wits. Mr. March was in the embrace of four pairs of loving arms; Jo nearly fainted away; Mr. Brooke kissed Meg; and Amy, having tumbled over a stool, hugged and cried over her father's boots. Mrs. March was the first to recover herself, and held up her hand, "Hush! Remember Beth is resting!"

But it was too late; the study door flew open, and Beth ran straight into her father's arms. Never mind what happened just after that, for the full hearts overflowed.

Soon, however, Mr. Brooke and Laurie left the family to itself for a time. Then Mr. March told how he had longed to surprise his girls and wife, and how when the fine weather came, he had been allowed by his doctor to take advantage of it, how devoted Brooke had been, and how good a young man he was.

There never was such a Christmas dinner as they had that day. The fat turkey was a sight to behold, when Hannah sent him up, stuffed, browned and decorated; so was the plum pudding, which quite melted in one's mouth. Everything turned out well.

Beth ran into her father's arms.

Mr. Laurence and his grandson dined with them, also Mr. Brooke. Two easy chairs stood side by side at the head of the table, in which sat Beth and her father, feasting modestly on chicken and a little fruit. They drank toasts, told stories, sang songs and had a thoroughly good time. A sleigh ride had been planned, but the girls would not leave their father; so the guests departed early and, as twilight gathered, the happy family sat together round the fire.

"Just a year ago we were groaning over the dismal Christmas we expected to have. Do you remember?" asked Jo.

"Rather a pleasant year on the whole," said Meg.

"I think it's been a pretty hard one," observed Amy.

"I'm glad it's over, because we've got you back," whispered Beth, who sat on her father's knee.

"Rather a rough road for you to travel, especially the latter part of it. But you have got on bravely, and I think the burdens are bound to tumble off very soon," said Mr. March. Meg was sitting beside him, and he took her hand that lay on the arm of his chair, and pointed to the roughened forefinger, a burn on the back, and two or three hard little spots on the palm. "I remember a time when this hand was white and smooth, and your first care was to keep it so. It was very pretty then, but to me it is much prettier now—for in these blemishes I read a little history. Meg, my dear, I value the womanly skill which keeps home happy more than white hands or fashionable accomplishments. I'm proud to shake this good, hardworking little hand, and hope I shall not soon be asked to give it away."

"What about Jo? Please say something nice, for she has tried so hard, and been so very, very good to me," said Beth, in her father's ear.

He laughed, and looked across at the tall girl who sat opposite.

"In spite of the short haircut, I don't see the 'son Jo' whom I left a year ago," said Mr. March. "I see a young lady who pins her collar straight, laces her boots nearly, and neither whistles, talks slang nor lies on the rug as she used to. She doesn't bounce, but moves quietly, and takes care of a certain little person in a motherly way. I rather miss my wild girl, but if I get a strong, helpful, tender-hearted woman in her place, I shall feel quite satisfied."

"Now, Beth," said Amy, longing for her turn, but ready to wait.

"There's so little of her, I'm afraid to say much, for fear she will slip away altogether, though she is not so shy as she used to be," began their father cheerfully; but recollecting how nearly he had lost her, he held her close, saying, with her cheek against his own, "I've got you safe, my Beth, and I'll keep you so, please God."

After a minute's silence, he looked down at Amy, who sat at his feet, and said, with a caress of her shining hair:

"I observed that Amy took drumsticks at dinner, ran errands for her mother all the afternoon, gave Meg her place tonight, and has waited on everyone with patience and good humor. I also observe that she does not fret much nor look in the mirror; so I conclude that she has learned to think of other people more and of herself less. I am glad of this, for I am infinitely proud of a lovable daughter with a talent for making life beautiful to herself and others."

A few moments later, Beth, slipping out of her father's arms, went slowly to the piano, and said, "It's singing time now, and I want to be in my old place."

So, sitting at the dear little piano, Beth softly touched the keys and, in the sweet voice they had never thought to hear again, sang to her own accompaniment an old hymn.

Chapter 11

Aunt March Settles the Question

L IKE BEES swarming after their queen, mother and daughters hovered about Mr. March the next day. But late in the afternoon, Meg was sitting sewing alone with Jo, when someone gave a tap at the parlor door.

"Good afternoon," said Mr. Brooke. "I came to get my umbrella—that is, to see how your father finds himself today."

"I'll get him," said Jo, "and tell him you are here."

The instant she vanished from the room, Meg began to go towards the door, murmuring, "Mother will like to see you. Pray sit down, I'll call her."

"Don't go; are you afraid of me, Margaret?" And Mr. Brooke looked so hurt that Meg thought she must have done something very rude. She blushed, for he had never called her Margaret before, and she was surprised to find how natural and sweet it seemed to hear him say it. She put out her hand, and said, "How can I be afraid when you have been so kind to Father? I only wish I could thank you for it."

"Shall I tell you how?" asked Mr. Brooke, holding her hand in both his own, and looking down at Meg with so much love in his brown eyes that her heart began to flutter.

"Oh no, please don't—I'd rather not," she said.

"I won't trouble you, I only want to know if you care for me a little, Meg. I love you so much, dear," added Mr. Brooke tenderly.

Meg hung her head and answered, "I don't know."

He pressed her hand and said, "Will you try and find out? I want to know so much, for I can't go to work with any heart until I learn whether I am to have my reward in the end or not."

"I'm too young," said Meg.

"I'll wait, and in the meantime, you could be learning to like me. Would it be a very hard lesson, dear?"

"Not if I chose to learn it, but—"

"Please choose to learn, Meg."

What would have happened next, I cannot say, if Aunt March had not come hobbling in at this interesting minute.

The old lady couldn't resist her longing to see her nephew. The family were all busy in the back part of the house, and she had made her way quietly in, hoping to surprise them. She did surprise two of them so much that Meg started as if she had seen a ghost, and Mr. Brooke vanished into the next room.

"Bless me, what's all this?" cried the old lady, with a rap of her cane, as she glanced from the young gentleman to the blushing young lady.

"It's Father's friend. I'm so surprised to see you!" stammered Meg.

"That's evident," returned Aunt March, sitting down. "But what is Father's friend saying to make you blush? There's mischief going on, and I insist upon knowing what it is."

"We were merely talking. Mr. Brooke came for his umbrella," began Meg.

"Brooke? That boy Laurie's tutor? Ah! I understand now. I know all about it. You haven't gone and accepted him, child?" cried Aunt March.

"Hush! He'll hear. Shan't I call Mother?" said Meg.

"Not yet. I've something to say to you, and I must free my mind at once. Tell me, do you mean to marry this man? If you do, not one penny of my money ever goes to you. Remember that, and be a sensible girl," said the old lady.

"I shall marry whom I please, Aunt March, and you can leave your money to anyone you like," she said.

"Highty tighty! Is that the way you take my advice, miss? You'll be sorry for it." Aunt March stared at her a few moments, and then began again in a softer tone. "Now, Meg, my dear, be sensible. I don't want you to spoil your whole life by making a mistake at the beginning. You ought to marry well, and help your family. It's your duty to make a rich match."

"Father and Mother don't think so; they like John, though he is poor."

"So you intend to marry a man without money, position or business, when you might be comfortable all your days by minding me and doing better? I thought you had more sense."

"I couldn't do better if I waited half my life! John is good and wise, he's got heaps of talent! He's willing to work, and sure to get on, he's so energetic and brave. Everyone likes and respects him, and I'm proud to think he cares for me, though I'm so poor and young and silly," said Meg.

"Well, I wash my hands of the whole affair. I'm disappointed in you, and haven't spirits to see your father now. Don't expect anything from me when you are married; I'm done with you forever!"

And, slamming the door in Meg's face, Aunt March drove off. When left alone, Meg stood a moment, undecided whether to laugh or cry. Before she could make up her mind, Mr. Brooke came into the room and embraced her, saying, "I couldn't help hearing, Meg. Thank you for defending me and proving that you do care for me."

"I didn't know how much till she insulted you," began Meg.

"And I needn't go away, but may stay and be happy, may I, dear?"

"Yes, John," she said.

Fifteen minutes after Aunt March's departure, Jo came softly downstairs, paused an instant at the parlor door and, hearing no sound within, walked in. It was a shock to see Mr. Brooke sitting on the sofa, with Meg upon his knee. Jo gave a sort of gasp. At the sound, the lovers turned and saw her. Meg jumped up, but Mr. Brooke laughed and said, "Sister Jo, congratulate us!"

Jo turned and rushed upstairs.

"Oh, *do* somebody go down quick; John Brooke is acting dreadfully, and Meg likes it!"

Mr. and Mrs. March left the room; and then Jo told the news

to Beth and Amy, who seemed pleased by it, rather than dis-tressed, as Jo was.

Nobody ever knew what went on in the parlor that afternoon, but a great deal of talking was done. Mr. Brooke pleaded his suit for Meg, told his plans and persuaded her parents to accept the situation.

It was a shock to see Mr. Brooke with Meg upon his knee.

That evening at supper, everyone looked very happy, and even Jo hadn't the heart to be jealous or dismal.

"You can't say nothing pleasant ever happens now, can you, Meg?" said Amy.

"The joys come close upon the sorrows this time, and I rather think the changes have begun," said Mrs. March. "In most families there comes, now and then, a year full of events; this has been such a one, but it ends well after all."

Laurie and his grandfather came over after supper, delighted with the news of the tutor's engagement with sweet Meg.

Noticing Jo's grim face, however, Laurie quietly asked her, "You don't look festive; what's the matter?"

"I don't approve of the match, but I've made up my mind to bear it, and shall not say a word against it," said Jo. "You can't know how hard it is for me to give up Meg."

"You don't give her up. You only go halves," said Laurie.

"It never can be the same again. I've lost my dearest friend," sighed Jo.

"You've got me, anyhow. I'm not good for much, I know, but I'll stand by you, Jo, all the days of my life; upon my word I will!" And Laurie meant what he said.

"I know you will, and I'm ever so much obliged. You are always a great comfort to me," returned Jo.

"Well, now, don't be gloomy. Meg is happy, Brooke will fly round and get settled with money soon, Grandpa will help him, and it will be very jolly to see Meg in her own little house. We'll have fine times after she is gone, for I shall be through college before long, and then we'll go on some nice trip."

"There's no knowing what may happen in three years," said Jo.

"That's true. Don't you wish you could take a look forward and see where we shall all be then?"

"I think not, for I might see something sad, and everyone looks so happy now," said Jo, and her eyes went slowly round the room.

Father and Mother sat together, quietly remembering their own first days of romance some twenty years ago. Amy was drawing a picture of the lovers, who sat apart in a beautiful world of their own. Beth lay on her sofa, talking cheerily with her old friend Mr. Laurence, who held her little hand. Jo lounged in her favorite low chair, with a serious, quiet look, and Laurie, leaning on the back of her chair, his chin on a level with her curly head, smiled and nodded at her in the long mirror that reflected them both.

Chapter 12

The First Wedding

THREE YEARS have passed and have brought but few changes to the quiet family. The war is over, and Mr. March safely at home, busy with his books and the small parish which found in him a fine minister. Mrs. March is as brisk and cheery, though rather grayer, than when we saw her last, and just now so absorbed in Meg's affairs that the hospitals and homes miss her visits.

John Brooke went off to the war for a year, got wounded, was sent home and not allowed to return. He devoted himself to getting well, preparing for business and earning a home for Meg. He accepted a job as a bookkeeper, not wanting to borrow money from generous Mr. Laurence.

Meg had spend the time in working as well as waiting, growing womanly, wise and prettier than ever. Jo never went back to Aunt March, for the old lady took such a fancy to Amy that she bribed her with the offer of drawing lessons from one of the best teachers; for the sake of this, Amy accepted. So she gave her mornings to duty, her afternoons to pleasure. Jo, meantime, devoted herself to writing and Beth, who remained delicate long after the fever was a thing of the past. She was never again the rosy, healthy creature she had been.

Laurie, having gone to college to please his grandfather, was now getting through it in the easiest possible manner.

And now let us speak of the "Dovecote." That was the name of the little brown house which Mr. Brooke had prepared for Meg's first home. Laurie had named it, saying it was just right for these gentle lovers, who "went on together like a pair of tur-

"Here I am, Mother!"

tledoves." It was a tiny house, with a little garden behind, and a lawn about as big as handkerchief in front.

"Are you satisfied? Does it seem like home, and do you feel as if you should be happy here?" asked Mrs. March, as she and her daughter went through the new kingdom, arm in arm.

"Yes, Mother, perfectly satisfied, thanks to you all." For her sisters and Laurie had just been helping her furnish and decorate it.

Just then, Jo cried out, "Laurie is coming!" and they all went down to meet the boy whose weekly visit was an important event in their quiet lives.

A tall, broad-shouldered young fellow, with a short haircut, came tramping down the road, walked over the low fence, straight up to Mrs. March, and, with both hands out, said, "Here I am, Mother!"

"Where is John?" asked Meg.

"Stopped to get the license for tomorrow, ma'am."

After more jokes and pleasantries, Laurie and Jo went off for a stroll.

"I do object to being seen with a person who looks like a young prize fighter," Jo scolded him.

"This haircut helps me study," returned Laurie. "By the way, Jo, and to change the subject, I think that Parker, my college friend, is really getting desperate about Amy. He talks of her constantly."

"We don't want any more marrying in this family for years to come," said Jo. "Mercy on us, what *are* the children thinking of?" And Jo looked as much scandalized as if Amy and Parker were not yet in their teens.

"It's a fast age, and I don't know what we are coming to, ma'am," teased Laurie. "You are a mere baby, but you'll go next, Jo."

"Nobody will want me. I'll be the old maid in the family."

"You won't give anyone a chance," said Laurie. "You get so thorny no one dares touch or look at you."

"I don't like that sort of thing. Now don't say more about it; Meg's wedding has turned all our heads, and we talk of nothing but lovers and nonsense."

As they parted at the gate of the house, Laurie said, "Mark my words, Jo, you'll go next."

The June roses over the porch were awake bright and early on that next morning. Meg looked very like a rose herself, for all that was best and sweetest in heart and soul seemed to bloom into her face that day, making it fair and tender.

As the younger girls stand together, giving the last touches to their simple outfits, it may be a good time to tell of a few changes which three years have made in their appearance, for all are looking their best just now.

Jo's angles are much softened, and she has learned to carry herself with ease, if not grace. The short haircut has lengthened into a thick coil. Beth has grown slender, pale and more quiet than ever; the beautiful, kind eyes are larger. Amy is with truth considered "the flower of the family," for at sixteen she has the air and bearing of a full-grown woman—not beautiful, but full of grace.

All three wore outfits of silver gray, with roses in their hair and on their chests; and all three looked just what they were—fresh-faced, happy-hearted girls.

The wedding took place in the Marches' home.

The wedding took place in the Marches' home, just as Meg wanted it. There was no bridal procession, but a sudden silence fell upon the room as Mr. March and the young pair took their places under the green arch they had fashioned for the occasion. Mother and sisters gathered close. Meg looked straight up in her husband's eyes, and said, "I will!" with such trust in her voice that her mother's heart rejoiced and Aunt March sniffed audibly.

After the wedding feast and dancing (even Mr. Laurence and Aunt March joined the dance), the young couple prepared to depart.

When Meg came down from upstairs, changed into a dove-colored suit and straw bonnet, they all gathered about her to say "good-by."

"Don't feel that I am separated from you, Marmee dear, or that I love you any the less for loving John so much," she said, clinging to her mother for a moment. "I shall come every day, Father, and expect to keep my old place in all your hearts, though I am married. Beth is going to be with me a great deal, and the other girls will drop in now and then to laugh at my housekeeping. Thank you all for my happy wedding day. Good-by!"

They stood watching her, with faces full of love and hope and pride, as she walked away, leaning on her husband's arm, with her hands full of flowers, and the June sunshine brightening her happy face—and so Meg's married life began.

Meg and John were very happy, even after they discovered they couldn't live on love alone. At first they played house, and frolicked over it like children; then John took to business, feeling the cares of the head of a family upon his shoulders; and Meg put on a big apron, and fell to work with energy.

It was a little more than a year later that there came to Meg a new experience—the deepest and tenderest of a woman's life. Meg had twins, a boy and a girl, the boy named John Laurence, after his father and also his patron, and the girl Margaret after mother and grandmother. They came to be known as Demi and Daisy.

Chapter 13

Calls

"COME, Jo, it's time," said Amy.

"For what?"

"You don't mean to say you have forgotten that you promised to make half a dozen calls with me today?"

"I don't think I ever was crazy enough to say I'd make six calls in one day, when a single one upsets me for a week."

"Yes, you did; it was a bargain between us. I was to finish the drawing of Beth for you, and you were to go properly with me, and return our neighbors' visits."

Jo hated calls of a formal sort, and never made any till Amy made her by use of a bargain, bribe or promise. In the present instance, there was no escape. Taking up her hat and gloves, she told Amy she was ready.

"Jo March, you are enough to provoke a saint! You don't intend to make calls in that outfit, I hope," cried Amy.

"Why not? I'm neat and cool and comfortable. If people care more for my clothes than they do for me, I don't wish to see them. You can dress for us both, and be as elegant as you please."

"Oh dear!" sighed Amy. "I'll do anything for you, Jo, if you'll only dress yourself nicely, and come and help me. I'm afraid to go alone; do come and take care of me."

"You're an artful little miss to flatter your cross old sister in that way. Well, I'll go if I must, and do my best. You shall be my commander, and I'll obey blindly; will that satisfy you?" said Jo.

"You're an angel! Now put on all your best things, and I'll tell you how to behave at each place, so that you will make a good impression. I want people to like you, and they would if you'd only try to be a little more agreeable."

When Jo was at last dressed according to Amy's order, Jo said, "I'm perfectly miserable; but if you consider me presentable, I'll die happy."

"Yes, you'll do."

"Am I to drag my best dress through the dust, or loop it up, ma'am?"

"Hold it up when you walk, but drop it in the house."

Jo sighed, as off they sailed away on their visiting.

"Now, Jo dear, the Chesters consider themselves very elegant people, so I want you to put on your best manners. Don't make any of your surprising remarks, or do anything odd, will you? Just be calm, cool and quiet—that's safe and ladylike, and you can easily do it for fifteen minutes," said Amy, as they approached the first place.

"Let me see, 'Calm, cool and quiet,'—yes, I think I can promise that."

Amy looked relieved, but naughty Jo took her at her word; for, during the first call, she sat unmoving, every fold in her dress correctly draped, calm as a summer sea, cool as a snowbank and as silent as a sphinx. In vain Mrs. Chester alluded to Jo's "charming story," and the Misses Chester introduced other topics, and each and all were answered by a smile, a bow and a modest "Yes" or "No." In vain Amy signalled the word "Talk," and tried to draw her out. But Jo sat on like ice.

"What a snobby, uninteresting creature that oldest Miss March is!" remarked one of the ladies as the door closed upon their guests.

When they were outside, Amy said, with disgust, "I merely meant you to be dignified, and you made yourself a perfect stone. Try to be sociable at the Lambs', gossip as other girls do, and be interested in dress and flirtations and whatever nonsense comes up. They move in the best society, and are valuable persons for us to know."

"I'll be agreeable, I'll gossip and giggle, and have raptures over any trifle you like. I rather enjoy this, and now I'll imitate what is called 'a charming girl.' See if the Lambs don't say, 'What a lively, nice creature that Jo March is!'"

Amy felt anxious, as well she might, for when Jo turned freakish there was no knowing where she would stop. Jo seemed possessed by the spirit of mischief, and talked away like mad, about matters that much embarrassed Amy; she was nearly as silly as the mother of the several Lamb young ladies and men.

"We read a story of yours the other day, and enjoyed it very much," observed the elder Miss Lamb, wishing to compliment Jo.

"Sorry you find nothing better to read. I write that rubbish because it sells, and ordinary people like it."

As Miss Lamb had "enjoyed" the story, this reply was not exactly grateful or complimentary. The moment it was made, Jo saw her mistake; but suddenly she remembered that it was for her to make the first move toward leaving, and so said, "Amy, we *must* go. *Good*-by dear; *do* come and see us; we are *pining* for a visit. I don't dare to ask *you*, Mr. Lamb; but if you *should* come, I don't think I shall have the heart to send you away."

Amy got them out of the room as rapidly as possible.

"Didn't I do that well?" asked Jo, as they walked away.

"Nothing could have been worse," was Amy's reply. "You never will learn when to hold your tongue and when to speak."

Poor Jo looked ashamed, and touched her nose with a handkerchief. "How shall I behave here?" she asked, as they approached the third mansion.

"Just as you please; I wash my hands of you," said Amy.

"Then I'll enjoy myself. The boys are at home, and we'll have a fun time. Goodness knows I need a little change, for elegance wears me out," said Jo.

A big welcome from three big boys and several pretty children made Jo feel better; and, leaving Amy to entertain the hostess, Jo devoted herself to the young folks, and found the change refreshing. She listened to stories, petted dogs, talked about books and looked at turtles.

As they left this family, Jo said, "Capital boys, aren't they? I feel quite young again after that."

The next family they were to visit were out, for which Jo was grateful, and Jo was again thankful when they reached the fifth house and were told that the young ladies were unavailable.

"Now let us go home, and never mind Aunt March today. We can run down there any time."

"Aunt likes to have us pay her the compliment of coming in style, and making a formal call; it's a little thing to do, but it gives her pleasure, and I don't believe it will hurt your things half so much as letting dirty dogs and clumping boys spoil them."

"What a good girl you are, Amy!" said Jo.

They found Aunt Carrol with the old lady.

They found Aunt Carrol with the old lady, both absorbed in some very interesting subject, but they dropped it as the girls came in. Jo was not in a good mood, and her mischievous spirit returned to her, but Amy kept her temper and pleased everybody. Both aunts "my deared" her affectionately, and felt what they afterwards said—"That child improves every day."

"Are you going to help about the fair, dear?" asked Mrs. Carrol, as Amy sat down beside her.

"Yes, Aunt. Mrs. Chester asked me if I would."

"I'm not," said Jo. "I hate to be patronized, and the Chesters think that it's a great favor to allow us to help. I don't like favors, as they oppress me and make me feel like a slave."

"Ahem!" said Aunt Carrol softly.

"I told you so," said Aunt March.

"Do you speak French, dear?" asked Mrs. Carrol, laying her hand on Amy's.

"Pretty well, thanks to Aunt March," replied Amy.

"How are you about languages?" asked Mrs. Carrol of Jo.

"Don't know a word. I'm very stupid about studying anything, can't bear French, it's such a slippery, silly sort of language."

A look passed between the ladies, and Aunt March said to Amy, "You are quite strong and well, dear?"

"I'm very well, and mean to do great things next winter, so that I may be ready for studying art in Rome, whenever that day arrives."

"Good girl; you deserve to go, and I'm sure you will some day," said Aunt March.

At this, Jo shook hands in a gentlemanly manner with the aunts, while Amy kissed them, and the girls departed.

As they vanished, Aunt March said, "You'd better do it, Mary; I'll supply the money."

And Aunt Carrol replied, "I certainly will, if her father and mother consent."

A week later a letter came from Aunt Carrol, and Mrs. March's face lit up when she read it. Jo and Beth, who were with her, demanded to know what the glad tidings were.

Amy began to pack that evening.

"Aunt Carrol is going to Europe next month, and wants—"

"Me to go with her!" burst in Jo.

"No, dear, not you; it's Amy."

"O mother! It's *my* turn first. I've wanted it so long."

"I'm afraid it's impossible, Jo. Aunt says Amy. And I'm afraid it is partly your own fault, dear. When Aunt spoke to me the other day, she regretted your blunt manners and spirit; and here she writes: 'I planned at first to ask Jo; but as "favors burden her," and she "hates French," I think I won't venture to invite her.'"

"Why can't I learn to keep quiet!" groaned Jo.

"Jo, dear, I'm very selfish, but I couldn't spare you, and I'm glad you are not going quite yet," whispered Beth, embracing her.

Amy received the news with great joy, and began to sort her paints and pack her pencils that evening.

"It isn't a mere pleasure trip to me, girls," Amy said. "It will decide my career; if I have any genius, I shall find it out in Rome."

It was not very long before Amy was off. On the steamer, and just as the gangway was about to be withdrawn, it suddenly came over Amy that a whole ocean was soon to roll between her and those who loved her best, and she clung to Laurie, the last lingerer from her family's farewell group, saying with a sob, "Oh, take care of them for me, and if anything should happen to Beth—"

"I will, dear, I will; and if anything happens, I'll come and comfort you," whispered Laurie, little dreaming that he would be called upon to keep his word.

Chapter 14

Consequences and a Secret

FOR SOME time, Jo had been forming plans of her own. She went to her mother one morning and told her, "I need stirring up, so, as you can spare my help this winter, I'd like to hop a little away and try my wings."

"Where will you hop?"

"To New York. I had a bright idea yesterday, and this is it. You know Mrs. Kirke wrote to you for some respectable young person to teach her children? I think I should suit her needs."

"What are your reasons for this sudden fancy?"

"It may be vain and wrong to say it, but—I'm afraid—Laurie is getting too fond of me."

"Then you don't care for him in the way it is evident he begins to care for you?"

"Mercy, no! I love the dear boy, and am immensely proud of him; but as for anything more, it's out of the question."

The plan was talked over in a family council, and agreed upon, for Mrs. Kirke gladly accepted Jo and promised to make a pleasant home for her.

When Laurie said good-by, he whispered, "It won't do a bit of good, Jo. My eye is on you, so mind what you do, or I'll come and bring you home."

From New York, Jo wrote volumes of letters to dear Beth and Marmee. We will skip over her many observations of New York, and her successful writing for newspapers and publishers, and instead quote a few lines of her first impressions of one of the several people living in Mrs. Kirke's boardinghouse:

"This afternoon, while doing some needlework, I heard someone humming like a big bumblebee. I lifted the curtain to the parlor, and saw there Professor Bhaer. While he arranged his books, I took a good look at him. A regular German—rather heavy, with brown hair tumbled all over his head, a bushy beard, the kindest eyes I ever saw and a splendid big voice. His clothes were old, his hands were large and he wasn't handsome at all, but had beautiful teeth. The children love him. I watched

"I saw there Professor Bhaer."

as he let them play with him—not only Mrs. Kirke's children, but also the ironing-woman's little girl."

As the weeks went on, she mentioned the dear professor more and more often. In exchange for Jo's darning his socks, he began to give her German lessons.

Why everybody liked him was what puzzled Jo, at first. He was neither rich nor great, young nor handsome; in no respect what is called fascinating or brilliant; and yet he was as attractive as a nice fire, and people seemed to gather about him as naturally as about a warm hearth. He was poor, yet always appeared to be giving something away; a stranger, yet everyone was his friend; no longer young, but as happy-hearted as a boy; plain and peculiar, yet his face looked beautiful to many. Jo often watched him, trying to discover his charm, and, at last, decided that it was kindness which worked the miracle. She felt proud to know, through one of the boardinghouse's gossips, that Professor Bhaer was an honored professor in Berlin, though only a poor language teacher in America.

It was a pleasant winter and a long one, for Jo did not leave Mrs. Kirke till June. Everyone seemed sorry when the time came; the children were so sad, and Professor Bhaer's hair stuck straight up all over his head, for he always rumpled it wildly when disturbed.

"Going home? Ah, you are happy that you haf a home to go in," he said.

She was going early the next morning, so she told him, "Now, sir, you'll come and see us, if you ever travel our way, won't you? I want my family to know my friend."

"Do you? Shall I come?" he asked.

"Yes."

That night, Professor Bhaer said to himself, "It is not for me; I must not hope it now." He had fallen in love with Jo, but could not believe that she would have love for him.

Jo returned home, in time to attend Laurie's graduation ceremonies from college.

Laurie was proud of himself, and as they took a walk one morning, Jo said, "Now you must have a good long holiday."

"I intend to."

Something in his voice made Jo look quickly at him. The moment she had feared had come. She put out her hand and said, "No, Laurie, please don't!"

"I will, and you must hear me. It's no use, Jo, we've got to have it out, and the sooner the better for the both of us. I've loved you ever since I've known you; couldn't help it, you've been so good to me. I've tried to show it, but you wouldn't let me; now I'm going to make you hear, and give me an answer, for I can't go on so any longer."

"I went away to keep you from doing this if I could."

"I thought so; but it was no use. I only loved you all the more, and I worked hard in college only to please you, and I gave up everything you didn't like, and waited, for I hoped you'd love me, though I'm not half good enough—"

"Yes, you are, you're a great deal too good for me, and I'm grateful to you, and so proud and fond of you, I don't see why I can't love you as you want me to. I've tried, but I can't change the feeling. Oh, Laurie, I'm sorry, so desperately sorry! You'll see that I'm right, by and by, and thank me for it—"

Laurie rushed away.

"I'll be hanged if I do!" said Laurie.

"Yes, you will!" persisted Jo. "You'll get over this after a while, and find some lovely girl who will adore you and make a fine wife for your fine house."

Laurie rushed away, suffering the biggest disappointment of his life.

When Jo came home that June, she had been struck with the change in Beth. No one spoke of it, but to Jo's eyes, sharpened by absence, it was very plain.

Laurie and his grandfather soon set off for Europe, on a trip meant to heal the young lover's wounds. With peace returned, Jo proposed to Beth a trip to the seashore, where she could live much in the open air, and let the fresh sea breezes blow a little color into her pale cheeks.

One day, as they were resting by the shore on the warm rocks, Beth saw that Jo had figured out her secret.

"Jo, dear, I'm glad you know it. I've tried to tell you, but I couldn't. I've known it for a good while, and now I'm used to it. Don't be troubled about me, because it's best; indeed it is."

"Is this what made you so unhappy in the autumn, Beth?"

"Yes, I gave up hoping then."

"O Beth, and you didn't tell me, didn't let me comfort and help you! How could you shut me out, and bear it all alone? Nineteen is too young. Beth, I can't let you go. I'll work and pray and fight against it. I'll keep you in spite of everything; there must be ways, it can't be too late. God won't be so cruel as to take you from me," cried Jo.

"I have a feeling that it was never intended I should live long. I'm not like the rest of you; I never made any plans about what I'd do when I grew up; I never thought of being married, as you all did. I couldn't seem to imagine myself anything but stupid little Beth. I never wanted to go away, and the hard part now is the leaving you all. I'm not afraid, but it seems as if I should be homesick for you even in heaven."

Jo could not speak, and for several minutes there was no sound but the sigh of the wind and the lapping of the tide.

"Amy is coming in the spring," said Jo finally, "and I mean that you shall be ready to see and enjoy her. I'm going to have you well and rosy by that time."

"Jo, dear, don't hope any more. It won't do any good, I'm sure of that."

When they got home, Father and Mother saw plainly, now, what they had prayed to be saved from seeing. Tired with her

Her father stood leaning his head against the mantelpiece.

short journey, Beth went at once to bed, saying how glad she
was to be at home, and when Jo went downstairs to her parents, she found that she would be spared the hard task of
telling Beth's secret. Her father stood leaning his head on the
mantelpiece, and did not turn as she came in; but her mother
stretched out her arms as if for help, and Jo went to comfort
her.

Chapter 15

New Impressions

At THREE o'clock in the afternoon, all the fashionable world at Nice, France, may be seen on the Promenade des Anglais—a charming place, for the wide walk, bordered with palms, flowers and tropical shrubs, is bounded on one side by the sea, on the other by the grand drive, lined with hotels and villas, while beyond lie orange orchards and the hills.

Along this walk, on Christmas Day, a tall, handsome young man walked slowly, with his hands behind him.

"O Laurie, is it really you?" called out a young, blonde lady. "I thought you'd never come!"

"I was detained on the way, Amy, but I promised to spend Christmas with you, and here I am."

After so many months of traveling and trying to forget Jo, Laurie was happy to see a face which reminded him of what he so dearly missed. Indeed, he found Amy more admirable than ever. She was as lively and graceful as ever, with the addition of elegance. Always mature for her age, she had gained a composure which made her seem more of a woman. Laurie was happy to spend the day with her, first feeding peacocks, and then driving up and around the hills. When finally he took his leave of her, he promised to return in the evening to escort her to a Christmas ball.

Amy deliberately primped that night, saying to herself, "I do want him to think I look well, and tell them so at home."

Truly, Laurie thought her unusually attractive that night, as he accompanied her to the Christmas party. Before the evening was half over, he had decided that "little Amy" was going to make a very charming woman.

Amy did not know why he looked at her so kindly, nor why he filled up her dance card with his own name and devoted himself to her for the rest of the evening in the most delightful manner, but the reason for this change between them was the result of the new impressions which both of them were giving and receiving.

Laurie went to Nice expecting to stay a week, and remained a month. He and Amy took comfort in each other's company, and were much together riding, walking, dancing or dawdling.

Laurie thought that the task of forgetting his love for Jo would absorb all his powers for years; but, to his great surprise, he discovered it grew easier every day.

One day, in his room, he glanced up at a picture of Mozart and thought: "Well, he was a great man; and when he couldn't marry one sister he took the other, and was happy."

Let us leave Laurie and Amy for a moment, and return to dear Beth.

The pleasantest room in the house was set apart for her, and in it was gathered everything that she most loved—flowers, pictures, her piano, the little worktable and the beloved cats. Father's best books found their way there, mother's easy chair, Jo's desk, Amy's finest sketches; and every day Meg brought by her babies, to make sunshine for Aunty Beth. John brought the fruit she loved; old Hannah never wearied of cooking nice little dishes to tempt her; and from across the sea came little gifts and cheerful letters from Amy and Laurie.

Cherished like a saint, Beth was as calm and busy as ever, for nothing could change the sweet, unselfish nature, and, even while preparing to leave life, she tried to make it happier for those who remained behind. The feeble fingers were never idle as she knit little gifts for children and friends.

The first few months were very happy ones, and Beth often used to look round, and say "How beautiful this is!" as they all sat together in her sunny room, the babies kicking and crowing on the floor, mother and sisters working near, and father reading in his pleasant voice.

It was well for all that this peaceful time was given them as preparation for the sad hours to come; for, by and by, Beth said the needle was "so heavy," and put it down forever; talking wearied her, faces troubled her, pain claimed her for its own. Ah me! such heavy days, such long, long nights, such aching hearts, when those who loved her best were forced to see the thin hands stretched out to them, to hear the bitter cry, "Help me, help me!" and to feel that there was no help.

Jo never left her for an hour since Beth had said, "I feel stronger when you are here." She slept on a couch in the room, waking often to renew the fire, to feed, lift or wait upon the patient creature who seldom asked for anything.

So the spring days came and went, the sky grew clearer, the earth greener, the flowers were up fair and early, and the birds came back in time to say good-by to Beth, who, like a tired but trustful child, clung to the hands that had led her all her life.

As Beth had hoped, death came easily, and in the dark hour before the dawn, lying on her mother's bosom, she quietly drew her last breath, with no farewell but one loving look, one little sigh.

The sad news met Amy at Vevey, for the heat had driven her and Aunt Carrol from Nice in May, and they had traveled slowly to Switzerland. She bore the news well and quietly submitted to the family orders that she should not shorten her visit, for, since it was too late to say good-by to Beth, she had better stay and let absence soften her sorrow. But her heart was very heavy; she longed to be at home, and every day looked across the lake, waiting for Laurie to come and comfort her.

He did come very soon; for the same mail brought letters to them both, but he was in Germany, and it took some days to reach him. The moment he read it, he packed his knapsack and was off to keep his promise to Amy.

When he arrived, Amy ran to him, exclaiming, "O Laurie, Laurie, I knew you'd come to me!"

I think everything was said and settled then, for, as they stood together quite silent for a moment, Amy felt that no one could comfort and sustain her so well as Laurie, and Laurie decided that Amy was the only woman in the world who could fill Jo's place and make him happy.

Over the next several days, in spite of the new sorrow, it was a very happy time, so happy that it took Laurie a little while to recover from his surprise at the rapid cure of his first and, as he had believed, last and only love. However, he soon had the conviction that it would have been impossible to love any other woman but Amy.

When Amy and Laurie wrote of their engagement, Mrs. March feared that Jo would find it difficult to rejoice over it, but her fears were soon set at rest; for, though Jo looked grave at first, she took it very quietly, and was full of hopes and plans for "the children."

"I am glad Amy has learned to love him," said Jo.

Chapter 16

Surprises

Jo was alone in the twilight, lying on the old sofa, looking at the fire and thinking. Her face looked tired, and rather sad, for tomorrow was her birthday, and she was thinking how old she was getting. Almost twenty-five, and nothing to show for it.

"An old maid," she said to herself, "that's what I'm to be. A literary spinster, with a pen for a husband and a family of stories for children."

Suddenly, Laurie's ghost seemed to stand over her. It was too real to be a ghost—"O my Laurie!"

"Dear Jo, you are glad to see me, then?"

"Glad! Of course. And where's Amy?"

"Your mother has got her down at Meg's. We stopped there by the way, and there was no getting my wife out of their clutches."

"Your what?" cried Jo. "You've gone and got married!"

"Don't I look like a married man?"

"Not a bit, and you never will. Why didn't you let us know?"

"We wanted to surprise you."

"That you have. I sincerely congratulate you. For now, after all, you really are my brother!"

The next day, on her birthday, a sudden sense of loneliness came over Jo, in spite of her family celebrating the day with her. But then there came a knock at the porch door.

She opened it, and started as if another ghost had come to surprise her, for there stood a tall, bearded gentleman, beaming on her from the darkness.

"O, Mr. Bhaer, I *am* so glad to see you!"

"And I to see Miss March—but no, you haf a party—" and the professor paused as the sound of voices and the tap of dancing feet came down to them.

"No, we haven't, only the family. My sister and friends have just come home, and we are all very happy. Come in, make one of us."

There stood Professor Bhaer.

"If I shall not be Mister Too-Many, I will so gladly see them all. You haf been ill, my friend?"

"Not ill, but sad. We have had trouble since I saw you last."

"Ah, yes, I know. My heart was sore for you when I heard that!" and he shook hands again.

When she brought him upstairs, she announced, "Father, Mother, this is my friend, Professor Bhaer."

He received a very kind welcome, and they liked him right

away. By the end of the evening, even Laurie thought him the most delightful old fellow he ever met.

"Please remember, sir," said Laurie to him, "that there is always a welcome waiting for you next door."

The professor thanked him, and then turned to Mrs. March, and said, "I must go, but I shall gladly come again, if you will allow me, dear madame. A little business in the city will keep me here some days." He spoke to Mrs. March, but he looked at Jo; and the mother's voice gave as kind an invitation as did the daughter's eyes.

When he had gone, Mr. March said, "I suspect that he is a wise man."

"I know he is a good one," said Mrs. March.

"I thought you'd like him," said Jo.

While Laurie and Amy were setting up house and planning their future, Mr. Bhaer and Jo were enjoying walks along muddy roads and soggy fields.

By the second week, everyone knew perfectly well what was going on, yet everyone tried to look as if they were blind to the changes in Jo's face. They never asked why she sang about her work, did up her hair three times a day and go so blushing red with her evening exercise of walks; and no one seemed to notice that Professor Bhaer, while talking philosophy with the father, was giving the daughter lessons in love.

For two weeks, the professor came and went with loverlike regularity; then he stayed away for three whole days, and made no sign—which caused everybody to look serious, and Jo to become thoughtful, at first, and then—alas—very cross.

"Disgusted, I dare say," said Jo to herself. "It's nothing to me, of course; but I *should* think he would have come and bid us good-by, like a gentleman," she said to herself, as she put on her things for the customary walk, one dull afternoon.

"You'd better take the umbrella, dear; it looks like rain," said her mother.

"Yes, Marmee; do you want anything in town? I've got to run and get some paper."

Mrs. March gave her a list of several items, and said, "If you happen to meet Mr. Bhaer, bring him home to tea. I quite long to see the dear man."

While in the city, it started to rain—and she found she had forgotten the umbrella. With packages in her arms, she rushed across one street, narrowly escaping being run over by a cart; but in doing so, she stumbled into Mr. Bhaer.

"Who is this strong-minded lady who goes so bravely under many horse noses, and so fast through much mud?" he teased her. Then he noticed how wet she was, and said, "You haf no umbrella. May I go with you, and take for you the bundles?"

"Yes, thank you."

She found herself walking arm in arm with her professor, his umbrella over her but feeling as if the sun had suddenly burst out, that the world was all right again.

"We thought you had gone," said Jo.

"Did you believe that I should go with no farewell to those who haf been so heavenly kind to me?" he asked.

"No, *I* didn't; I knew you were busy about your business, but we rather missed you—Father and Mother especially."

"And you?"

"I'm always glad to see you, sir."

"I thank you, and come one time more before I go. I haf no longer business here; it is done. My friends find for me a place in a college, where I teach."

"How splendid!"

"Yes, but this place is at the West."

"So far away!"

"Miss March, I haf a great favor to ask of you," began the professor.

"Yes, sir."

"I am bold to say it in spite of the rain, because so short a time remains to me."

"Yes, sir."

"Heart's dearest, why do you cry?"

"Because you are going away!"

"Ach, mein Gott, that is *so* good!" cried Mr. Bhaer. "Jo, I haf nothing but much love to gif you; I came to see if you could care for it, and I waited to be sure that I was something more than a friend. Am I? Can you make a little place in your heart for old Fritz?"

"Oh, yes!" said Jo.

The professor looked as if he had conquered a kingdom, while Jo trudged beside him in the rain, feeling as if her place had always been there.

"What made you stay away so long?" she asked.

"It was not easy, but I could not find the heart to take you from that so happy home until I could haf a prospect of one to gif you, after much time, perhaps, and hard work. How could I ask you to gif up so much for a poor old fellow, who has no fortune but a little learning?"

"I'm glad you are poor; I couldn't bear a rich husband," said Jo. "And don't call yourself old—forty is the prime of life." She kissed her Fritz under the umbrella.

Then, turning from the night and storm and loneliness to the household light and warmth and peace awaiting them, with a glad "Welcome home!" Jo led her lover in and shut the door.

For a year Jo and her professor worked and waited, hoped and loved, met occasionally and wrote many letters. The second year began, and Aunt March died suddenly. But when their first sorrow was over—for they loved the old lady in spite of her sharp tongue—they found she had left her immense house, lavish garden and fruitful orchards to Jo, which made all sorts of joyful things possible.

Jo announced, "I want to open a school there, a school for little lads—a happy, homelike school, with me to take care of them and Fritz to teach them! Now, thanks to my good old aunt, we can live at Plumfield perfectly well, if we have a school. It's just the place for boys."

It was a very astonishing year altogether, for things seemed to happen in an unusually rapid and delightful manner. Almost before she knew where she was, Jo found herself married and settled at Plumfield. Then a family of six or seven boys sprang